"We left someone!"

It was an all-out retreat, everyone crashing into everyone, and everything, else, and at least two guys stepped on Michael before he got enough nerve to start crawling away himself. There was still so much machine-gun fire that he was afraid to lift his head at all. An RPG thudded into a tree somewhere above his head, and splintered wood and leaves, and shrapnel, landed all over the place, Michael rolling into a ball to try and protect himself.

Was he okay? He was okay. Jesus! He started crawling again, then heard a voice screaming for help somewhere behind him. He stopped, looking around wildly, trying not to lift his head more than a couple of inches off the ground.

"Sarge!" he shouted at the top of his lungs. "Sarge!"

Sergeant Hanson came back in a swift high-crawl.

"We left someone!" Michael said.

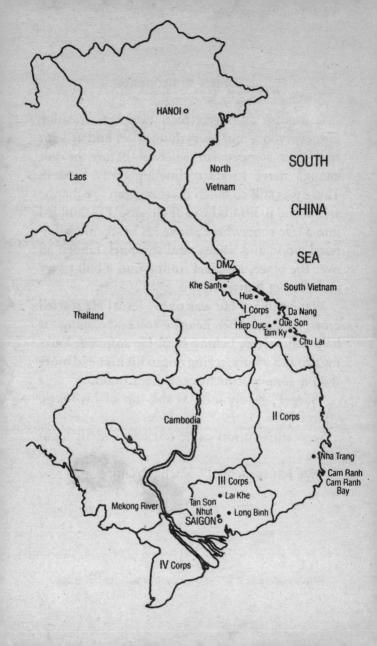

ECHO COMPANY

#2

HILL 568

ZACK EMERSON

SCHOLASTIC INC.
New York Toronto London Auckland Sydney

ISBN 0-590-44592-8

12 11 10 9 8 7 6 5 4 3 2 1   1 2 3 4 5 6/9

Printed in the U.S.A.   01

First Scholastic printing, September 1991

For Walter Pitkin, to whom I owe a lot.

This is a work of fiction, based on fact. Although certain actual locations and unit designations are used, incidents are meant to be representative of activity going on in Vietnam during this time span.

HILL 568

CHAPTER 1

THAT NIGHT, Michael couldn't keep his dinner down. That night, after that day. Every *second* he'd spent in Vietnam so far — hard to believe it hadn't even been two weeks yet — had been a nightmare, but today had been — beyond imagination. Not that he was real big in the imagination department, but — Jesus.

Who would have imagined that a guy could be standing there, one second, and then be blown into — the guy was *talking* when it happened — and a second later, the only thing left was — pieces. Nothing that could ever have been human. Could ever have been alive. It had been like something out of — Dante's Butcher Shop.

And no one knew what to do. Even the guys who were *supposed* to know. It was so sudden, so catastrophic, that everyone just stood there. The only person who moved was Snoopy, who threw up. J.D., the guy who had been killed, was

3

one of the veterans — he'd been in-country for over eight months. He was one of the best in the platoon — always walked point when they were on patrol, made everyone else feel safe — and now, somewhere in Iowa, an Army car was pulling up in front of a farmhouse, and J.D.'s parents were going to look out the window, and know why those solemn-faced men had come, before they even opened the front door. Sir, Ma'am, I regret to inform you that your son James . . .

C-rations tasted so terrible going down, it was hard to believe that they tasted even *worse* coming back up.

"You okay, Meat?" a voice behind him asked. Hesitantly. Snoopy. Michael had only known him for a few days, but they shared a foxhole, they shared food — and in a place where people were alive one second and dead the next, Michael was already too close to him. Probably too late to do anything about it, too. You couldn't stop being friends with a guy just because you were afraid he was going to go and die on you. Or, hell, maybe you could. Should.

"You okay?" Snoopy asked, again.

Did he *look* okay? "Yeah," Michael said, and wiped his mouth on his sleeve. Meat. If he'd hated the damned nickname before, he hated it even more now. Until today, he'd never realized how close to the truth it was. For all of them. Thinking about that made him sick again, and he turned his face away, trying to throw up quietly. Not that there was much left inside to come up, at this point.

When he was finished, he sat up, wrapping his arms around himself, having to fight not to cry. He was ten thousand miles away from home, in the middle of the jungle, surrounded by people he barely knew — and they all might be attacked and killed at any given second. He just wanted to be *home*. Safe. Have his mother bring him a tray with ginger ale and Saltines.

"Rinse out, man," Snoopy said, still behind him, handing over a canteen.

The water in Vietnam tasted awful, and he almost threw up again, but he managed to slosh it around his mouth a little, then spit it out. Didn't help much.

"Want some gum?" Snoopy asked.

Gum. Michael laughed weakly.

"Sounds like a yes, from my little friend Meat," Snoopy said, and handed him a piece, then took one himself.

Automatically, Michael put it in his mouth. "You're smaller than I am," he said — also automatically. He and Snoopy were definitely the smallest guys in their squad — and probably the whole platoon. Kind of embarrassing.

"You *wish*," Snoopy said, in his best tough-kid-from-Newark voice.

"I *know*," Michael said, and chewed his gum. Chewed hard. It didn't make him feel better.

They sat there. Tonight, the whole company — Echo Company — was together, so Lieutenant Brady told them to dig three-man foxholes. He and Snoopy were sharing with Finnegan — a dark-haired Irishman who had been J.D.'s best friend. Who was — no surprise — in pretty bad shape right now.

"How's he doing?" Michael asked, gesturing over his shoulder.

Snoopy just shook his head, and Michael knew that that meant that Finnegan was still sitting in their hole, crying. Not that he was the only guy who had been doing some crying this afternoon. Michael wasn't much for crying — wasn't very good at it — but he would have preferred it to throwing up. Didn't seem like he was getting much choice in the matter.

It wouldn't be dark for about an hour yet, so people were still digging in for the night, cleaning their weapons, heating up C-rations for dinner. Michael should have known better than to even *try* eating dinner — with visions of blood and literal guts dancing in his head. Although there were guys out beyond the perimeter pulling guard duty, the atmosphere was pretty casual. If grim. GIs own the day, VC own the night, as the saying went.

In the hole next to theirs, Jankowski, the squad's radio man, was still digging with fierce energy. Again, preferable to throwing up. Viper was presumably out on guard, and Michael had no idea where Sergeant Hanson was. Although Lieutenant Brady was technically in charge of 1st Platoon, it was Hanson who really ran the show. Hanson, who was only a year or two older than the rest of them. Hell, the *Lieutenant* was twenty-two, twenty-three, at the most.

It was hot — in Vietnam, it even seemed hot when it *rained* — but Michael felt kind of cold, and he shivered once. His t-shirt was too big, and he looked at the sleeves, wondering if he should cut them off, instead of letting them hang halfway to his elbows and look stupid. Except — did he really care how he looked? Out here, in the middle of the jungle, where they were all perpetually filthy and disgusting? *Stables* smelled better. Lots better.

Truth was, it wasn't even his t-shirt. When J.D. — blew up — poor Finnegan had been right next to him. Had gotten covered with — stuff. Nobody had seemed to know what to do, and Michael hadn't, either, but he knew someone had to clean the poor guy off — *fast*. Finnegan's shirt was such a mess, Michael couldn't get the stuff off, so he cut it off him and put his shirt on Finnegan instead. It was filthy, but at least there wasn't any blood on it.

Then, when they were in the LZ, waiting for the dust-off to come pick up the body bag, Michael had been standing there, in his flak jacket and no shirt, when some guy from Three Squad — Michael didn't even know his name — came up to him with an extra t-shirt. "You did good, man," was all the guy said, shoved the shirt into his hands, then went back to join his squad. Michael felt tired, and sick, and confused, so he just put it on, about three sizes too big.

"I'm real sorry," Snoopy said, breaking the silence.

Michael looked up. "What?"

Snoopy, normally one of the happiest-looking guys you could ever hope to see, looked guilty. Kind of like a puppy. "I fucked up," he said. "Let you down."

Michael shook his head, and looked out at the jungle. He couldn't see much. Didn't mean they weren't out there.

"I should've helped you," Snoopy said, and looked about as sick to his stomach as Michael still felt. Gum or no gum. "I just — I *couldn't*, Meat. I couldn't touch — " He shivered. "I'm real sorry. You mad at me?"

Michael shook his head. He was about as far as you could get from a volunteering-type of guy — real, *real* far — but someone had had to, so he did. Made sense at the time. Hell, even Sergeant Hanson had been standing there, looking young, and numb.

"I should've helped," Snoopy said, unhappily. " 'Stead of Viper."

Thank God for Viper. Who didn't talk much — Michael had no idea where he was from, or really anything about him — but just when he thought he was going to have to do this awful job alone, Viper was right there behind him. Had some advice about not making friends you couldn't stand to lose, too.

But — Michael didn't want to think about that. At the moment. Truth was, he didn't want to think at all.

"So, you mad at me?" Snoopy asked, still looking worried, and unhappy.

"I will be if you don't shut up," Michael said.

Snoopy nodded, and shut up, and they chewed their gum.

*   *   *

They were still sitting there when they heard a stern voice behind them.

"Oh, great," Snoopy muttered. "Kendrick."

"Who's he?" Michael asked, glancing back. Big burly guy, reddish face, huge neck and shoulders, surprisingly high voice.

"New L-T, 3rd Platoon," Snoopy said. "Total prick."

"You there," Kendrick was saying, "soldier. You call that a hole?"

Finnegan. He was picking on Finnegan. Michael got up instantly, heading over.

"I *asked* you a question," Kendrick said.

Bastard. Finnegan was sitting all huddled up in the bottom of the foxhole — obviously in, like they said, a world of hurt — and this guy was giving him abuse.

"The man had a real bad day," Michael said, quietly.

Kendrick scowled at him. "Did I ask for your opinion, private? There's a war going on — he's going to have a lot of bad days."

Michael scowled right back. "His best friend fucking blew up all over him today. Leave him alone."

"What's your name, soldier?" Kendrick asked. He was probably trying to bark it, but with the high voice, it was more of a yip. To Michael's ears, anyway.

"Meat," Michael said, and spit. Pretty close to Kendrick's jungle boot. "They call me Meat." Behind him, he heard Snoopy suck in an uneasy breath, but — hell with it. Like he really cared about the chain of command? Not hardly.

The lieutenant stared at him, then returned his attention to Finnegan. "You," he ordered. "Go down another foot, and I want to see some grenade sumps in there, too. Before we lose the light. Move it!"

Finnegan, pale and shaky, slowly got up, reaching for an entrenching tool. Kendrick nodded once, gave Michael a hard look, then turned to walk away.

Only — this wasn't over yet. Not a chance. "Hey, *bud*," Michael said after him. A pretty damned good bark, actually.

Kendrick spun around. "What?!"

"You heard me," Michael said, dimly aware that someone else was hustling over. Had to be Sergeant Hanson. No one else was that alert.

"All right," Kendrick said, and a muscle somewhere near his jaw twitched. "That's just about enough. You have any idea who I am? You've just talked yourself into — "

"I don't care if you're Westmoreland's little

brother," Michael said. General Westmoreland was the commander in chief of all troops in Vietnam. "You got a lot to learn about human decency."

"Well, let me tell *you* something, *bud,*" Kendrick started, his face even redder.

"Hey, there," Sergeant Hanson was suddenly next to them — between them, really — calm as a man could be. "Anything wrong, L-T?"

"Yeah," Kendrick said. "You've got a real insubordinate little son-of-a-bitch here."

"Well, I'll take care of it, L-T," Sergeant Hanson said, calmly. "You can be sure of that."

"I *am* going to be sure of it," Lieutenant Kendrick said, scowling. "Starting with an Article Fifteen and — "

"Then what are you going to do?" Michael asked. "Send me to Vietnam?" He spit again. Damn close, this time. "Big shot college boy. Excuse me while I go puke some more." He climbed into the foxhole, took the entrenching tool from Finnegan, and started digging.

"I'll handle it from here, L-T," Sergeant Hanson said. Calm, calm, calm. "I think they're looking for you at the CP, anyway." He reached down, hauled Michael — not gently — out of the foxhole, then plucked the shovel out of his hands and gave it to Snoopy. "Go at least another foot, Snoopy," he said, one hand still tightly twisted in the back of Michael's shirt. He looked at Lieutenant Kendrick. "Really, sir. Everything's under control."

Kendrick scowled, but strode away.

Sergeant Hanson gave Michael a push. Not gently. "You and I are going to take a little walk now, Meat," he said.

They took a little walk. Sergeant Hanson was so dangerously silent that Michael was kind of intimidated. Okay. A *lot* intimidated.

Once they were out of everyone's earshot, Sergeant Hanson stopped, swept the jungle with his eyes, then focused on Michael. Silently.

Michael studied the jungle, too — like he would have any idea what to do if the entire NVA came walking right up to them. But — one of them was going to have to break down and say something, and, yeah, it was going to have to be him. Sergeant Hanson hadn't even *blinked* yet.

Okay. Michael sighed. "He started it, Sarge. He's a total — jerk." To say the least.

"Yeah," Sergeant Hanson said, "so?"

"So he was picking on Finnegan," Michael said, defensively.

Sergeant Hanson was still staring him down. "So?"

"So I told him to cut it out," Michael said.

Sergeant Hanson frowned. "We may be out in the bush, but an officer's still an officer. Still in charge."

"Yeah?" Michael looked right at him, folding his arms across his chest. "So where were *you* this afternoon?" Oh, hell. He hadn't planned on saying that. *Damn* it.

"Failing to do my duty," Sergeant Hanson said, after a pause, his voice very stiff. "Which I don't need some damn arrogant little cherry to point out to me."

There was a long silence while they looked at each other, then — quickly — looked out at the jungle. At this particular point in time, having the NVA walk up would *lighten* the atmosphere.

"I'm sorry, Sarge," Michael said. "I didn't mean to be disrespectful."

Unexpectedly, Sergeant Hanson laughed. "You just spit at an officer back there, Mike. That's, uh, that's pretty disrespectful."

"*He* doesn't deserve my respect," Michael said.

Sergeant Hanson shrugged. "Maybe, maybe not. But, you're in the Army, and no matter who the man is, you have to respect the rank."

"I don't want to be in the Army," Michael said. Automatically.

"Gee — really, Mike? I never would have guessed that." Sergeant Hanson grinned again. "Gee."

Michael had to grin, too.

"And you're right about today," Sergeant Hanson said, more serious. Much more serious. "Next time, I'll — I just — " He let out his breath, suddenly looking like a twenty-year-old kid in over his head instead of a rough, tough platoon sergeant. "He was a good friend," he said quietly.

Michael nodded. "I'm sorry. I didn't mean to say anything. It was stupid."

"Well. Better said than unsaid." Sergeant Hanson let out his breath again, hard, then looked over. "Are the two of us going to have problems? Regularly?"

Michael shook his head. "No, sir."

"I'm a 'sergeant,' not a 'sir,' " Sergeant Hanson said.

"Yes, sir," Michael said, and grinned a little.

Sergeant Hanson grinned a little, too. "Well. Excuse me," he gave the phrase some extra irony, "while I go get your butt out of the sling you put it into." He gave Michael a hard punch in the arm, then turned to go.

"Ow." Michael looked under the flopping t-shirt sleeve to see if there was a bruise. "That hurt."

Sergeant Hanson grinned. "It was supposed to," he said, and walked away.

CHAPTER 2

STANDING THERE, alone, Michael decided to check the claymore mines he and Snoopy had set out. They were still facing forward — always kind of a good idea, since the alternative meant pretty certain death — and he moved one slightly to improve their field of fire. Improve its probable killing force. Great. Job well done. His parents would be so proud.

His gum tasted awful — sour — and he spit it out. Spit a couple more times for good measure. Might be a nice new habit. Like smoking, and drinking coffee, and shooting at people. All the new things that he did, now that he was in Vietnam. Normally, he only spit when he was playing baseball — and that was just for show. And, spitting aside, the inside of his mouth still tasted like a moldy old penny someone had tossed into a compost heap, and left there for a very long time. Tasted swell.

When he finally walked back to their foxhole, Snoopy was actually hard at work digging a grenade sump — making the bottom of the foxhole slope down to a little trench that, in theory, a thrown grenade would roll into, and the damage would be minimized. Far as Michael was concerned, if someone threw a grenade into the foxhole while they were in it, they were just plain screwed. Be a perfect end to a perfect day.

Snoopy stopped digging, paused significantly, then spit right near Michael's boot. Well — *on* Michael's boot. Okay, that was kind of funny. Michael grinned, and even Finnegan smiled.

"Sarge was pissed, hunh?" Snoopy said.

Michael nodded.

"You in trouble?"

Michael frowned. "Hard to say."

Finnegan, sitting on a sandbag at the edge of the hole, staring down at a limp lit cigarette, looked up. "Don't guess you'll make general," he said.

Michael sat on another sandbag, next to him. "Colonel's good enough for me." Finnegan's cigarette smelled good — comparatively speaking — and Michael lit one of his own. He was getting so he didn't even cough much anymore.

What was left of his C-rations was still on the ground near the hole, and just looking at the cans made him feel sick again. He was going to kick them out of sight — especially the remaining meatballs and beans — but decided he'd better salvage some of the rest of the stuff. The pound cake, in particular. Pound cake was considered just about the best C-ration thing you could get, and guys generally saved it until they were lower than low. He started to put the little can in his rucksack, stopped, and held it out to Finnegan.

"I'm not all that hungry," he said. "Want my pound cake, man?"

Finnegan looked over dully.

"*I* want it," Snoopy said, digging.

"Didn't offer it to you," Michael said.

Finnegan kept smoking. No smoke rings. Before today, Finnegan — and, yeah, J.D. — had always been starting smoke ring blowing contests. "He can have it," he said. "I'm not hungry, either."

Michael pulled Finnegan's rucksack over, and stuffed the can into it. "Well, save it for later."

Finnegan smiled a little, and smoked.

"You, um, want my peaches, too?" Snoopy asked, holding a can out with almost-convincing enthusiasm. "For a 'specially good treat?"

Treat. Michael grinned. Didn't know one way

or the other, but he got the feeling Snoopy had a lot of sisters. Or maybe he just kept rereading *Little Women* or something.

Finnegan shook his head.

"Well — you best take it anyway," Snoopy said, and put the can in Finnegan's rucksack. With brave enthusiasm. Then, he sat up on the edge of the hole, and swung his legs a couple of times.

"Whatsa matter, little boy?" Michael asked. "Someone pop your balloon?"

Snoopy nodded sadly.

"Life's a bitch," Michael said, and smoked.

Snoopy nodded, and swung his legs again.

"You ever read *Little Women*?" Michael asked.

Snoopy frowned at him. "Hunh?"

"*Five Little Peppers*?" Michael asked.

"You're weird, Meat." Snoopy swung his legs. "Weird as hell."

It was going to be dark soon, and there wasn't a whole lot to say. Or do, really. War — boredom, and terror. Didn't seem to be much in-between.

Doc Adams, the platoon medic, came jittering over, stopping in front of Michael. A guy who looked seventeen — *tops*.

"Heard you was sick, kid," he said.

Kid. "I was sick," Michael agreed, and let out some smoke.

Doc's frown was always somewhere between extreme concern and considerable impatience. "You still sick?"

Sort of. His stomach sure as hell *hurt*. Michael shrugged.

Doc looked him over, looked at all of them, then sighed. "All right, all right, all right." He fumbled inside his medical bag and came out with a can of Coca-Cola.

Michael sat up straighter in spite of himself. Tempted, in fact, to yank it right out of his hand. He *loved* Coke.

"It's very warm," Doc said.

Be mature. Don't grab it. Don't knock him down. "That's okay," Michael said, trying not to sound eager.

"Damn right it's okay," Doc said, and handed him the can.

"Thanks." Michael opened the can — fast — and took a warm gulp. It tasted *great*.

"Sip it slow now, hear?" Doc said. "Might settle your stomach."

Michael nodded, forcing himself to sip. It wasn't easy. "Want some?" he asked, to be polite. He didn't feel like being polite. Didn't feel like it at all.

Doc patted him on the head. "That's okay, kid. Drink up." He took out a crumpled bag of M&M's, shaking two into Michael's hand, and three each into Snoopy and Finnegan's hands. "Enjoy, kids," he said, and left.

He should share his Coke. It would be nice of him to share his Coke. He should be nice. He looked at Finnegan. "Want some?" he asked.

"*I* want some," Snoopy said.

Finnegan took the can, took a sip, handed it back.

"You want some more?" Michael asked.

Finnegan shook his head.

Michael looked at Snoopy, then handed him the can, more than a little grudging. "You suck the whole thing down, and I'll smack you about seven hundred times," he said.

Snoopy grinned, and took a very small sip. Then, he ate one of his M&M's in three small bites. "May I have another sip?" he asked, very sweetly.

Michael nodded. Grimly.

"Thank you," Snoopy said, sipped, and handed the can back.

Michael nodded, and took a large sip.

"I don't think he's going to share the rest of it with us," Snoopy said to Finnegan, who nodded, and ate a brown M&M.

"Right the first time," Michael said, and kept sipping.

When it was dark, Snoopy volunteered to take the first watch, and Michael didn't argue, pulling his poncho liner out of his rucksack. Finnegan was already wrapping himself in his own liner, and curling up in the bottom of the foxhole. He was very quiet, and Michael hoped he had already fallen asleep. The guy needed it.

Michael took off his flak jacket, and folded it to use as a pillow. Only — what if they got mortared, or a grenade went off, or — he thought better of the idea, put the flak jacket back on, covered himself with his poncho liner, and lay down, using his arm as a pillow. He pulled his M-16 right over next to him, felt in the darkness to make sure that it was loaded, and that the safety catch was on, then closed his eyes.

Coke or no Coke, he still felt pretty damned sick.

They were supposed to switch off every two hours, but when Snoopy woke him up, it had been — by Michael's bleary-eyed squint at his watch, covering the lighted dial with his hand — four hours.

"It's late," he whispered. "Can't people in Newark tell time?"

"Cut ya some slack, babe," Snoopy whispered back.

Oh. "Thanks," Michael said.

Snoopy didn't answer, possibly already asleep. He had a reputation for being able to fall asleep even before he had time to close his eyes. Michael had seen him live up to that reputation.

Speaking of which. Even with the two extra hours sleep, Michael was exhausted. He propped his M-16 up in the firing position they'd formed with their sandbags, and felt in the pitch-darkness for the claymore detonators. Checked his grenades, his two flares, made sure they were where he could get to them in a hurry. Extra ammo, too. Then, he leaned his weight on his elbows, on the ground above the hole, doing his best to stay awake.

It was very quiet. Hard to believe that there were seventy, eighty guys spread out all around him. Every now and then, he could hear artillery — defending some other platoon or company? Harassment and Interdiction fire? — hard to say. He thought he heard gunships at one point, and wondered if the guys who were out on night ambush had run into trouble. Well —

not a lot he could do about it, either way. Except, try to stay awake. Do his job here.

There were plenty of mosquitoes, having a snack at his expense, and he slipped his bottle of bug juice out of his helmet band, spreading some onto his face and neck and arms. Didn't seem to help much, but he was too tired to care. Too tired to be scared. Too tired to be much of anything.

He was trying to keep his mind clear — empty — but he couldn't help thinking. If only today, bad as it was, was as bad as it was going to get — but, he had a feeling that today was just an introduction to the level of horror in this stupid country. This war.

Fuck John Wayne, for making it seem so — glamorous. So filled with dignity, and scope, and — logic. Like everything had a point, and if you *did* die — and everyone else would see it coming a long way off, and be prepared — it was always heroically, neatly, and in a blaze of color and trumpeting soundtrack music.

Like hell.

And maybe the worst part was, even though he hadn't known J.D. long enough to see it in action, he knew from the way everyone looked up to him that J.D. *had* been a hero. More than

once. And what was the Army going to tell his
family — that the poor guy bought it while he
was trying to find a place to sit down? He hoped,
at least, that the Army would assure the family
that J.D. was cut down while trying to drag a
fellow soldier to safety, or while charging a
bunker or something. Not that he was tired, and
hot, and confused, and stepped on a mine by
accident. He deserved better than that.

Don't think about it. Watch the damn perimeter. Because if he thought about it, his — yeah,
his stomach was already starting up again. He
tried to think of something else. *Anything* else.
Being at home, and skiing; grabbing raw cookie
dough out of the bowl while his mother laughed
and slapped at his hand with the wooden spoon;
the way his dog, Otis, looked the day he saw
him quivering at the side of the road and made
his father turn the car around so they could go
back and pick the little stray up. Ever since, Otis
had brought new dimensions to the phrase "dog
your footsteps," following him everywhere.
Which he liked a lot.

Hadn't followed him here, of course. In fact,
with all of his other current problems, one little
nagging worry he'd had, ever since he'd stepped
on the plane to come over here, was that something would happen to Otis while he was gone,

his family would be afraid to tell him, and he would get home to find out that he had been hit by a car six months ago, or something. To the degree that he had made a dire threat to his brother Dennis before he left, telling him that he'd just *better* let him know if something terrible happened — or suffer the consequences.

When it came to dealing with his brother, he liked to make his threats ominous, but vague. Give himself room to maneuver. He was good at looking mean, and usually, the threats were enough in and of themselves. If not — well, smacking him worked okay, too.

Watch the goddamn perimeter. Only — his stomach was getting out of control. He swallowed. Hard. Don't throw up. This was *not* a good time to throw up. If there ever was. But, in a war, when they were supposed to be practicing noise discipline — that was a particularly bad time.

Did John Wayne ever throw up?

He had to think about something else. Stop flashing on this afternoon and what it had looked like when — he swallowed as hard as he could. Think. Watch. Keep it down. Think about *Elizabeth*, even. Oh, yeah, his favorite subject. Think about how stupid it had been to tell her he loved

her, since she was going to turn right around
and — now he really *was* sick.

Hell with it. Hell with *her*. Like he even cared.
But — he was really sick. And he didn't know
what to do. Had never thought to ask. He looked
out at the dark perimeter, tightly gripping the
M-16, gulping down the bile every time it threat-
ened to rise. Oh, help.

He thought he had it under control, but realized, almost as quickly, that he didn't. There
wasn't even enough time to wake up Snoopy
before he — he scrambled out of the hole, throwing up behind it, trying as hard as he could to
be quiet. What a way to give away their position.
Only, he was too sick to worry about it at the
moment. Just tried to be quiet.

Whoever was in the hole to their right — some
guys from Two Squad, he thought — heard the
noise and panicked, firing wildly into the jungle.
Then, everyone on this side of the perimeter was
firing, flares were going up, and at least one claymore was blown, noise thundering through the
night.

Snoopy and Finnegan were up and shooting —
and Michael was just trying to stop throwing up.
He heard an urgent voice hissing, "Hold your
fire!" and, after a few more seconds, it stopped,
except for a few final M-16 shots. "Hold your

goddamn fire!" the voice hissed. Lieutenant Brady. There were a lot of low whispers to his right and, pretty sure the vomiting was over, embarrassed as hell, Michael crawled back into his foxhole.

"Where *were* you?" Snoopy whispered, sounding mad. "We thought you — shit, I don't know *what* we thought!"

"I was getting sick," Michael whispered back.

"Should've stayed in the hole," Finnegan said.

"Oh, yeah, *right,*" Michael said, and wiped his mouth on his sleeve. They would have *loved* that.

"Next time, wake us up," Snoopy said, all of them still whispering. Attempting to salvage what was left of their noise discipline.

"Sorry." Michael swallowed a few times. "I was kinda busy."

Lieutenant Brady had crawled over to them now. "What was it?" he asked softly. "Any of you see anything?"

This was pretty damned embarrassing. "I think it was me," Michael said. "I was sick. Sorry."

There was a pause. "You all right now?" Lieutenant Brady asked.

Oh, yeah. He was super. "Yeah," Michael said, and hoped it was true.

There was another pause. "Full-alert for an hour, then trade off 'til first light," Lieutenant Brady whispered, then went crawling off to the next hole.

Great. Now, three whole platoons were losing sleep because *he* had a weak stomach. Damn. If they found out, they were going to hate him. Fucking new guy.

"Sorry," he whispered to Snoopy and Finnegan, all three of them facing out towards the perimeter, guns ready.

"It's cool. We pick up for each other, man," Finnegan whispered.

He still felt bad about it. Actually, he felt bad, period.

"You all right now?" Snoopy whispered.

Tough call. "I don't know," Michael whispered.

It was quiet, as Snoopy thought this over. "Try to miss me," he whispered.

"Do my best," Michael whispered back, and hunched over his gun, watching the perimeter, trying to keep his mind on anything else.

Even the war.

CHAPTER 3

By DAWN, it was raining. Everyone was wet. Everyone was tired. Everyone was miserable. A small patrol went out to see if they had managed to hit anything in all of the shooting — out of sheer dumb luck — but, it didn't look that way. Big surprise.

Michael felt too unsteady to eat, so he just drank some coffee. Sugar. No damn cream substitute. Mostly, guys saved their cream substitute for C-rat cocoa, anyway. Made it slightly less awful. Finnegan gave him a couple of crackers, and he forced them down. Doc came around with malaria pills, and he had to force that down too. On *good* days, malaria pills made him sick. The concept of a "good" day in Vietnam being pretty damned relative. Good being Purgatory, bad being Hell, maybe.

"Feeling any better, kid?" Doc asked.

Michael smiled weakly.

31

"If it gets worse, let me know," Doc said. "They might let me evac you out of here. But — ain't likely." He checked their names off his list for malaria pills, and went over to get Viper and Jankowski next.

Michael and Snoopy and Finnegan sat, in their ponchos, in the rain. They were supposed to fill in their hole, police the area, watch the perimeter, and so forth, but none of them had quite managed to summon the energy yet.

"We better get moving," Snoopy said.

Finnegan lit another cigarette, shielding it with his hand from the rain. "Yeah."

Michael just nodded.

Sergeant Hanson came over, looking a hell of a lot more awake than anyone else in the general area. Looked like he'd even shaved. Of course, there were a fair number of guys in the platoon who didn't even *need* to shave. Michael, unfortunately, among them.

"Better hustle up," Sergeant Hanson said. "We're pulling out at 0630." Then, he looked at Michael. "Got a minute, Meat?"

Oh, now what? Was he going to get yelled at for *throwing up*? Like he could help it. It was going to be one long goddamned year. Already mad, he got up, barely managing to resist the urge to spit. His swell new habit. Fuck authority, man.

"You still sick?" Sergeant Hanson asked. "Or you always look this bad in the morning?"

Well — no question that he felt pretty crummy. On the other hand, when he stumbled downstairs to breakfast at home, his little sister often said things like, "Hi, Poindexter," and giggled wildly. Like it was his fault he had cowlicks. "I don't know," he said, automatically touching his — very dirty — hair. "Little of both."

Sergeant Hanson nodded. "You get something to eat?" he asked.

What? Michael looked at him, intentionally widening his eyes and making his voice quaver. "Mom? Y-you seem so — tall."

"I'm not kidding, Meat," Sergeant Hanson said, although one side of his mouth came close to moving up. "You have to make yourself eat out here. Skinny kid like you, doesn't have a lot of weight to *lose*."

Kid. Christ. "Lean," Michael said. "Wiry."

"Whatever," Sergeant Hanson said. "Kid like Bear comes in, he can miss a few. Kid like you, we have to keep an eye on."

Bear — who *was* big — had come out to the field the same day he had. "Well. Anyway." Michael folded his arms. "You going to yell at me for last night?"

Sergeant Hanson frowned. "Thought it was Moretti started the shooting."

Oh. "Well, it was my fault," Michael said, and shifted his weight. Had he done something *else* wrong? That he didn't even know about?

Sergeant Hanson just shrugged. "I want to talk to you about something," he said.

If anything, it was raining even harder. "So, talk," Michael said, shrugging back.

Sergeant Hanson looked right at him. "We need a new point man. I don't mean the ones who switch off, I mean the one we can count on."

J.D. J.D. had been the main point guy in the platoon. The guy walking point walked first. Was responsible for finding booby traps, ambushes — was responsible for everything, really. If you got into trouble, it was probably because the point guy led you into it. And, because the point man went first, he was the most likely to be killed. The best target. In a war full of dangerous jobs, point was about as bad as it got.

"Meat?" Sergeant Hanson said.

Oh, Christ. Just what he didn't want. Like he didn't have enough problems just finding his way along already. Michael sighed, and rubbed some rain out of his eyes. Then, stopped abruptly, in case it looked like he was crying. He was — cranky, is what he was.

"Brady and I don't force anyone to do it," Sergeant Hanson said. "Lot of platoons do — even throw the new guys out there, let 'em sink or swim. *I* want a volunteer. A guy who's too scared isn't going to do anyone much good. Don't want a guy who's too cocky, either." He looked at Michael, and waited.

"So, I'm supposed to volunteer," Michael said, "or I'm chicken-shit."

Sergeant Hanson shook his head. "No. That's why I'm asking you privately. I want an honest answer."

Michael thought about it, looking at the rain. Was it letting up some? Maybe. Then again, maybe not. "Why me?" he asked. "There's plenty of guys, been here a helluva lot longer than I have."

Sergeant Hanson shrugged. "You're tough. You keep your head."

Hmmm. "How come you don't ask Snoopy or someone?"

"Too happy," Sergeant Hanson said, without hesitating. "You put a happy guy up there, he forgets and looks at a flower or something."

Michael nodded. He wouldn't want Snoopy

up front, anyway — he'd worry about him too much. At least if *he* were up front, it would always be his responsibility. His fault. He might kind of prefer it that way. The buck stops *here*, damn it. On the other hand —

"Think you'll be able to keep that temper under control?" Sergeant Hanson asked. "Can't have a point man going around half-cocked all the time."

"Oh my God." Michael looked down at his crotch. "Where's the rest of me?" Did Sarge watch old movies?

Sergeant Hanson laughed. "Maybe I should rethink this."

"You ever see that movie?" Michael asked. "With, you know, what's-his-name?"

Sergeant Hanson nodded.

"Dumb movie," Michael said. But, kind of okay. *King's Row*. His mother was always making them watch movies. Sunday afternoons, especially. His father had always said that he and Dennis and Carrie should, for Christ's sakes, go out and get some fresh air, but his mother thought movies were worth missing out on a little sunshine. And she would make popcorn, and let them drink Cokes.

"Pretty dumb," Sergeant Hanson agreed, then looked at his watch. "So?"

Right. Back to the war. "I'm not going to know what to look for," Michael said. "Probably get us all killed."

"If you're willing to learn, I'm willing to teach," Sergeant Hanson said. "We're not going to put you out there cold."

Good.

"So, we're agreed?" Sergeant Hanson said.

Shit. Point. Michael nodded.

"Okay," Sergeant Hanson said. "2nd Platoon's got the point today, so we'll worry about it later."

Terrific. Something to look forward to. Michael nodded.

"Okay. Take those claymores in," Sergeant Hanson said. "We're going to saddle up soon."

Michael nodded, blinking rain out of his eyes. *Damn,* he needed a boonie hat. A brim. Going to be a lot of fun, slogging through the mud today, waiting for someone to shoot at them. "Sarge?" he asked. "How many guys said no before you got to me?"

"None," Sergeant Hanson said.

Michael frowned at him. "You asked me *first*?"

Sergeant Hanson nodded.

Oh. How about that.

"Don't get cocky," Sergeant Hanson said.

Michael grinned. "Never happen," he said, and grinned again.

It rained all morning, and they walked all morning. Nothing much happened, except that they all got even more tired, and even more wet. The VC were probably sitting in their damned tunnels, nice and dry, eating lunch, and having a good laugh about the dumb, muddy Americans, walking around the jungle like there was some point to it all.

What was weird was, when the jungle was really thick — triple-canopy — the rain didn't even seem to get all the way down to the ground, but the jungle floor sort of — steamed. Creepy. And hot. And there were leeches *everywhere*. Especially on all of them. It was so wet that it was hard to get cigarettes lit, to burn the damned things off. It wasn't fair to waste their few cigarettes on leeches, either. If they didn't get resupply today, all of the smokers — which included just about everyone — were going to be in trouble. They all might even get — tense.

Tense? In Vietnam? No. Never happen.

Wet, the jungle smelled even worse than usual. Of overpowering rot. So far, it seemed like the most common smell in Vietnam was raw sewage, but this was — earthier — than that. Nature was

supposed to smell *good,* for Christ's sakes. Like
lilacs, and evergreens, and all. Like Bambi might
come bounding out any second. Hard to picture
Bambi in Vietnam. Bambi, all thin and sick and
limping.

What a stupid place. If he lived here, he'd be
fighting to get *out,* not to stay. Maybe he was
too American for his own damned good, but the
way to end this war might be to take all of the
North Vietnamese guys to the United States for
a vacation. Let them see what a *nice* place was
like. Seemed like, the *worst* place in America was
better than the *best* place here. The NVA would
start fighting for visas. Passports.

Could be, that was judgmental of him.

"Wake up," Jankowski muttered behind him.

Michael looked around, realized he was wandering a little, and picked up the pace, Viper too
far ahead of him. Intervals. They were supposed
to keep regular intervals. Some damned point
guy *he* was going to make.

The way their boots were all sucking in the
mud — the *gunk* — you'd figure every enemy
soldier within miles would be able to track their
exact route, and ambush at will. Unless, of
course, they were still snacking in their tunnels,
and listening to Hanoi Hannah rant and rave.
Rock and roll. Michael hadn't heard her yet, but

apparently she was always broadcasting over the radio, trying to ruin the morale of American fighting forces by talking about hamburgers and what everyone's girlfriends were doing with other guys back in the World. Listen up, American GI, I saw Elizabeth — *saw* her — in the cafeteria at UC/Boulder, making out with some long-hair.

Only — she wasn't his girlfriend. She hated him. She had only asked his mother for his address so she could send him some grief in writing. Continue to make his life a living hell.

Not that he cared. No way.

On top of that, GI, Hanoi Hannah would say, she went over to your house and kicked Otis. *Hard*. Made him yelp.

Wake up. Watch the damned trail. This was a war, not a nature hike. Don't think, don't pay attention to bugs and leeches, pretend not to be dizzy and exhausted, and almost collapsing under the weight of a rucksack that the Green Bay Packers would have trouble carrying.

He stumbled along, his M-16 slippery with rain — probably getting ready to jam on him, his helmet very heavy on his head. Slipping down over his eyes, more often than not.

FTA, man. FTA.

They were stopping. Thank God. They were

supposed to set up in a loose perimeter, and he could hear Sergeant Hanson saying something to that effect, but Michael pretty much fell down right where he was, too tired to do anything but take off the damned ruck, and collapse next to it.

Snoopy dragged himself over, sitting down next to him. Clumsily. Then, he winced. "You got one on your neck, man," he said, pointing.

Michael touched his neck, and felt a fat leech. Fat with *his* blood. And he was so tired he found this only moderately interesting.

"Can't *leave* it there," Snoopy said.

The hell he couldn't. "He's ugly, but he's got a nice personality," Michael said.

Snoopy laughed. "Knew a girl like that once."

"Don't doubt it," Michael said, and watched the muddy ground steam around him. Bake at 350° for several hours, basting in its own juices. If he didn't watch it, he was going to end up on the goddamn cover of *Woman's Day*. Roasted GI. Serve with crispy oven-browned potatoes, and green beans mixed with mushroom soup. Maybe a Jell-O mold, too. With cut-up bananas in it. Marshmallows.

"You asleep?" Snoopy asked.

Michael opened his eyes. "Not anymore."

"Just — get the fucking thing off, will you?"

Snoopy asked, opening a can of turkey loaf, cutting his thumb slightly on the lid. "It's making me sick."

Michael looked over. Didn't seem to be hurting his appetite, any. Cold wet turkey loaf, for Christ's sakes. But, he squirted some bug juice on the leech and tried to pull it off. It didn't want to go. Seemed fond of him. Too bad he couldn't tell all those elementary school teachers who had written on his report cards that Michael is an extremely sensitive little boy who seems to have trouble making friends. Maybe they'd be impressed by this very close, very *fat* new friend.

Viper leaned over with a lit cigarette. Michael nodded, burned the leech off, then handed the cigarette back. Viper nodded, too, and went back to smoking.

"Good," Snoopy said, chewing away. "You was makin' me *sick*."

The thought of cold, wet turkey loaf was making *him* sick. Sick*er*. Michael closed his eyes again. "Wake me up if a battle starts," he said.

"Yep," Snoopy said, and kept eating.

CHAPTER 4

HE GOT — maybe — ten, fifteen minutes of sleep before the order came to saddle up. It took a few seconds to figure out where he was, then he staggered to his feet, groggy as hell.

"Your ruck, man," Snoopy said.

Oh. Michael looked down at it, wet and lumpy on the ground, frags and C-rat cans tied up in soggy socks hanging off it. The thought of bending down was so tiring that he just kept looking down at it, swaying a little on his feet. Usually, they tried to lean their rucks up against trees, so they would be easier to put on later, using the trees to pull themselves up.

"Come on, Meat, we gotta get moving," Finnegan said, and lifted the rucksack up, helping him put it on.

Michael nodded, shrugging his shoulders a few times to try and get it to rest comfortably. If such a thing were possible. Then, he rubbed his hand across his eyes, still feeling half-asleep and thick-headed.

They were walking again. Stumbling. Slogging. Vaguely downhill, climbing over and around rocks. Michael fell a couple of times. Tore his pants the first time, bruised hell out of his knee the second time. Landed so hard it was a damned good thing they kept the rifles on safety. He was too tired to be embarrassed, and besides, it was so muddy, other guys fell down sometimes, too.

They walked and walked and walked. Downhill for a while longer, then uphill for a much longer time. Seemed that way, anyway. The rain stopped, and now it was just plain damned hot again, the ground drying a hell of a lot faster than seemed possible. They all went from rain-drenched to sweat-drenched in no time.

It was so hot that they stopped more often, Doc jittering around to make sure everyone was taking salt pills, and one of the times, a small group of guys was sent off to a nearby stream to top off as many canteens as they could carry.

Michael still felt too sick to eat, and spent the rest breaks lying down with his eyes closed. Doc had to give him a kick to make him sit up enough to gulp down some salt pills. Little pink things that made you feel sicker than you already did.

"You best eat something, ya jerk," Doc said. " 'Fore you up and pass out."

Michael nodded, and lay back down, covering his face with his helmet. He *hated* this war. Hated it a lot. Hated everything about it.

Jankowski pushed a canteen cup of C-rat coffee into his hands and Michael held it tightly, making himself drink some. The hot metal burned against his hands, but the pain helped him wake up a little.

Snoopy and Thumper — a lanky former football player in Two Squad — were sprawled out on the ground nearby, joking around as they looked at a wet, muddied issue of *Playboy*. Looked like the magazine had seen better days. And not recently.

"Bet she's real brainy," Thumper said thoughtfully, studying the centerfold.

"I like that," Snoopy said. "A girl with smarts. Never spend time with nothing but."

Okay. He couldn't let that one go by without a comment. Michael sat up all the way. "How come it hasn't rubbed off?" he asked.

"Oh, but it surely has," Snoopy said. "I learn *them* stuff, not the other way around."

Michael leaned over to have a look. Most of the water damage was in exactly the wrong places. Although, if she were a shy girl — somehow, he didn't get that impression — she would probably be relieved by this. "She read poetry?" he asked. "Like they always do?"

"Yep," Snoopy said. "Sure does. Like I said, the young lady here is *smart*."

"I think that I shall never see, a poem as lovely as a tree," Michael said, and lay back down. Stupid thing to say. They were going to think he was some kind of damned book guy. Not *this* GI. No, sir.

Thumper looked at Snoopy. "Don't know 'bout that boy," he said.

Snoopy nodded. "White boys. They surely are not like you and me."

" 'Bout ten times uglier," Thumper said.

"Ten *thousand*," Snoopy said.

Michael tried to drink some of his coffee lying down and spilled a bunch on his chest. Snoopy and Thumper thought this was pretty funny. Michael thought it was pretty painful.

"Okay, boys," Sergeant Hanson said, striding past them, like he'd never been tired a day in his life. "Get ready to move out."

Snoopy held up the *Playboy*. "What do you think, Sarge?"

Sergeant Hanson examined it briefly. "I think she probably has to lean forward when she walks," he said, and handed it back. "Let's saddle up, okay?"

Snoopy and Thumper looked at each other.

"Married guys," Snoopy said, and shook his head.

"They ain't no fun," Thumper agreed.

Michael sat up, watching Sergeant Hanson go down the column, waking people up and getting them ready to go. "He's married? Isn't he kind of young?"

Thumper shrugged, cracking open his M-79 to check it, then standing up. "Lots of these guys're married. Fish, Garcia, that L-T in 3rd Platoon."

Kendrick was married? Hard to believe someone would *choose* to spend a lifetime with him. Michael drained the canteen cup, wiped it off with the cleanest part of his t-shirt — which wasn't very — then handed it to Jankowski, who nodded and stuffed it into his ruck.

"Viper's got a baby, even," Snoopy said.

Well, that explained why Viper always got so many letters. But, boy, he was pretty young, too. With an effort, Michael slipped his arms into his rucksack straps, then pushed against the tree behind him to get up. Yeah, it really was easier that way. It was pretty foul though, because his

skin seemed to be wearing away right where the
straps dug in. From all the weight, or was it
some kind of awful jungle rot starting? He didn't
even want to think about it. Hurt like a bitch,
too.

"Not even two more klicks, boys," Sergeant
Hanson said, moving back up the column, making sure everyone was on their feet and ready to
go. "Look alert."

"Uphill or downhill, Sarge?" Finnegan asked.

Sergeant Hanson grinned wryly, and kept
moving past them.

Uphill. Great.

The hill where they set up their NDP had apparently been used before, so they didn't have
as much work as usual — cleaning out old positions rather than digging new ones. They were
getting resupply, so one detail went to work
clearing the new growth away from the old LZ,
while two other details — including Michael's
squad — started digging positions for the two
sixty millimeter mortars the weapons platoon
was humping. Michael figured there was safety
in numbers, so they were probably better off
patrolling with the whole company, but when
the weapons platoon was along, they all had to
carry artillery rounds. Share the burden. Just one

more heavy thing to carry. And he didn't even want to think about what would happen if a stray bullet hit the round while he was carrying it. Not that he wasn't carrying plenty of ammo and explosives of his own.

"With Weapons here now, and this much diggin' in, they might let us stay here a couple days," Snoopy said, throwing a shovelful of dirt — mud, really — into the sandbag Michael was holding.

It was full, so Michael tied it off, then stacked it on the wall they were building. Parapet, actually. Seemed sort of stupid to be putting up more protection for a couple of little mortar guns than they were going to have for themselves, but, hey. Lieutenant Brady said do it, so they were doing it. Lieutenant Brady was an okay guy.

"So, think we'll get to stay?" Snoopy asked, for about the tenth time.

Viper shrugged. "Could be," he said, and kept digging.

"I think we will," Snoopy said, and then, instead of dumping his next shovelful in the fresh bag, he dumped it all over Michael's pants. He laughed. "Sorry."

Oh, yeah. Real sorry. "Just fill the damn thing," Michael said. "We've still got our own hole to fix."

"We surely do," Snoopy agreed, and tossed another shovelful all over him.

What a jerk. Michael stood there for a second, like he wasn't going to react, then jammed the sandbag over Snoopy's head, holding it just tightly enough so that he wouldn't be able to get it off — and finding this quite hilarious, as Snoopy struggled. Then, Snoopy kicked him and Michael used his other leg — the one that didn't hurt — to sweep his feet out from underneath him. They ended up in the mud, wrestling, both having a pretty good time. It had been a lousy day.

Someone was hauling them apart, swearing, and Michael knew — just *knew* — it was going to be his friend Lieutenant Kendrick. Which, of course, it was.

"The hell's going on here?" he demanded, his face bright red and perspiring. Then, he scowled at Michael. "Oh. *You* again."

Much as he disliked officers, this was probably a good time to keep his mouth shut, so Michael just nodded. Snoopy pushed the sandbag up, looking sheepish, keeping it on as a little hat. Looking, in fact, like an Eighth Dwarf named Muddy.

"It was my fault, L-T," Snoopy said. "It was a tough hump, and I was just playing around."

Kendrick ignored him completely, staring at Michael. "You know what a poor excuse for a soldier you are, troop?"

Michael nodded, then hung his head. Sometimes, penitence impressed officers. Kendrick did not seem impressed. So, Michael put his hands in his pockets, and just stood there looking pleasant. It was an effort, but it was hard to yell at someone who looked pleasant.

"You're looking for it, soldier," Kendrick said grimly. "You know that?"

"Yes, sir," Michael said. Pleasantly. "I look, and I look, and — " He shook his head. "It's driving me mad, sir."

Kendrick looked at him, then gave the wall a hard kick, sandbags spilling off and into the mud. "Start over, and do it right," he said. "Square 'em off."

Sure. Fine. Whatever he wanted. Fuck it. Michael set his teeth, and bent down to pick up the sandbags and put them back in place. He had only just started when Kendrick kicked them off again.

"I said do it *right*," Kendrick said.

They were in the bush. Officers weren't supposed to screw around with them in the bush. Too many short-tempered guys standing around with loaded weapons, for one thing. Michael counted to ten. Twice. "You're pushing *me*, sir," he said, calmly. "Not the other way around. If you write it up, write the truth." Then, he bent to pick up the bags again. He hefted two of them up onto the wall, square as can be, then folded his arms, looking at Kendrick dangerously. Daring the guy to fuck with him some more.

"Better," Kendrick said, finally, and walked away.

Michael was going to flip him off, or spit, or something, but he hated to do stuff like that behind someone's back. He'd a hell of a lot rather look them straight in the eye first. Make sure they knew he meant it.

"Take it easy, Meat," Viper said, still digging away. He probably hadn't even paused the whole time. "You got 'most a year yet."

Right. Michael nodded. "Someone *married* that guy," he said. "Guess that means there's hope for all of us." Then, he gritted his teeth, and stacked the rest of the spilled sandbags.

It turned out, 1st Squad was going out on ambush right after sundown, so they all decided it was more important to spend some time eating, and resting up, than it was to do a great job on foxholes they weren't even going to use. They were going to be out all night. If Snoopy was right, and they were going to hold this position for a couple of days, they could always fix the holes better tomorrow.

Resupply came in with more ammo, C-rats, water, and a guy in a battered cowboy hat who was back from R & R in Bangkok. Wasn't much of a surprise to hear people calling him Tex. The chopper didn't bring any beer, but they did bring enough cases of 7-Up for everyone to have a can. There wasn't any hot food, so everyone was mad, but there *was* a fat red nylon bag of mail, so everyone was instantly less mad. Doc handed it out, full of comments and remarks about various letters that smelled of various perfumes. The guys lucky enough to get letters like that seemed to enjoy these remarks. Doc came across one envelope, his expression changed slightly, and he put it in his pocket, before handing out the rest with slightly less energy. The pink envelope looked just like the ones J.D.'s girlfriend always sent, and Michael figured that the stupid guys back in the rear who sorted the mail hadn't gotten the word yet.

"Hey, Meat." Doc tossed him an envelope. "Looks like Mommy's checkin' in."

All right. Michael grinned, and went over to

his shallow foxhole to read it. Viper had two letters, Jankowski and Finnegan each had one, and Snoopy didn't have any. Didn't look too happy about it either, just sitting on the side of their hole, drinking his 7-Up.

Michael sat down next to him. "Going to read over my shoulder again?"

Snoopy grinned. "Yep."

"No rude comments," Michael said, slitting open the envelope.

"Nope," Snoopy said, and grinned again.

Michael pulled the letter out — stationery with an American flag waving in the corner — taking his time. This was definitely the best thing that had happened all day, and there was no point in rushing it. He had written home, but only a few days ago, and it wouldn't have gotten there yet. So, she was probably pretty worried.

Dear Mike,

We still haven't heard from you, but I'm sure it must take a long time for a letter to come from someplace so faraway. I know it's silly, but I keep the television on almost all day, in case there's any news. It's so hard having you gone, and I just can't get anything done for worrying.

Damn. He should have written her before he got out to the field, so she would have it by now.

It upsets your father to look at Mr. Cronkite during dinner, so he stays down at the station late, and we eat when he gets home.

All of this made Michael feel pretty homesick, and he lowered the letter for a minute.

"Your family sounds nice," Snoopy said, his voice a little wistful and homesick, too.

Michael nodded, looking down the hill at the tangle of jungle.

"Come on, man." Snoopy pushed his arm. "Let's read the rest."

Michael nodded, and lifted the letter.

We're seeing some snow clouds in the sky, but we haven't really gotten any yet. Otis's coat is getting real thick, so I guess we're in for a tough winter. Your father says he's just growing all that fur so he'll have more to shed. Anyway, Otis is just fine, but I know he's waiting for you to come home as much as I am. I keep finding him sleeping up on your bed. He's ruining your grand-

mother's afghan, but he's so sweet, I don't have the heart to kick him off.

"Is Otis your brother, or what?" Snoopy asked.

"You're not supposed to make smart remarks," Michael said.

"Right," Snoopy said, and drank some 7-Up.

Reverend Champlin had us say a prayer for you and the Morris boy and the rest of the boys over there last Sunday. He's at a place called Quang Tri — I don't know if that's near you or not. His mother's real worried about him, but says he's supposed to be home in February. After the service, a lot of people came up. I guess they hadn't even known that you were over there. It's hard to believe, since I can't think of anything else.

Not much news here. Carrie got a guitar from Gail's sister, and she's practicing every day. Your father says we just aren't musical, and I'm afraid he's right, but Carrie is still strumming away. Dennis says he's going to go into her room and cut the strings to shreds while she's asleep. Your father may beat him to it, but I'm sure she'll lose in-

*terest soon, anyway. When you think that
we have that nice old upright of your grand-
father's and not a one of us can play it.*

"Did they make you take piano lessons?"
Snoopy asked.
Michael nodded.
"Were you terrible?"
Michael nodded and kept reading.

*Dennis made the basketball team, but
then he wouldn't run his laps —*

Big surprise. Dennis's attitude was about a
hundred times worse than his was.

*— so now he's spending all his time
down at the station, trying to get that blue
Studebaker running. Your father says that
if he can fix it, it's all his, but I wish he
would spend more time on his studies. He's
really such a smart boy, but he just won't
work at it.*

Not that Michael ever had either, but at least,
he usually kept his mouth shut about it. Showed
up to class, sat in the back, got B's, left it at that.
Kept a low profile.

I sent you a package with some special
things you might like, but if there's anything
you need, you just write, and your father
and I will find it for you. Please make sure
you eat — you know I worry. I hope you
know how proud your father and I are of
you. We all miss you, and I pray for you
every day. Please be careful, and be safe.

Love, Mom

Michael looked at the letter for a long time,
so homesick that his throat hurt.

"They really do sound nice," Snoopy said,
breaking the silence.

Michael nodded.

"Hope I can meet 'em someday," Snoopy said,
kind of shyly.

Michael nodded, folding the letter neatly, and
putting it in the empty ammo can where he kept
things he wanted to stay dry, and safe. "Hope
you can, too," he said.

CHAPTER 5

HIS MOTHER wanted him to eat, so Michael decided to eat, after going to collect his can of 7-Up, and grabbing a few boxes of C-rats to share with Snoopy. While he was at it, he stole an extra 7-Up for him, too. There seemed to be plenty left. The crates of C-rations had been pretty well picked over, but as far as he was concerned, all C-rats tasted pretty lousy, so it didn't make much difference which ones he got. Ham and limas were, for sure, the worst though.

Walking back over to their hole, he tossed one of the boxes to Snoopy. "More turkey loaf for you," he said.

"Mmm, boy," Snoopy said cheerfully, and ripped the cardboard open.

Michael put the rest of the boxes down on the ground, taking — after a long pause to decide — chopped ham and eggs for himself. He just wasn't up for meatballs and beans today. If ever.

"Know what makes it better?" Snoopy asked, setting up the little blackened C-rat can he used for a stove, small vent holes punched in the sides. "Dump some out, then melt up your cheese spread and stir it in. Buncha pepper too."

Michael thought about that. Okay. He could maybe even pretend the crackers from his crackers and cheese were toast. He was pretty fond of toast. His mother thought cocoa and thickly buttered cinnamon toast was the only snack worth having while watching late night movies. He had never found any reason to disagree with this.

They heated up their dinners, and drank warm 7-Up. Despite still feeling a little sick, Michael was hungry enough so that he didn't have too much trouble getting the ham and eggs down — and the melted cheese really did improve the taste. Maybe he could get his mother to send him some dried onions, or garlic or something. That'd help even more.

They were both eating cans of fruit cocktail when Lieutenant Brady came wandering over. Although he was very tall, there was something frail about him and, as always, he looked as if he needed a shave. On the other hand, Michael had seen him in the morning, right after he'd shaved, and even then, his skin was so pale and his beard was so dark, that he *still* looked like he needed one.

"How you two doing?" Lieutenant Brady asked.

Snoopy drank the juice left over from his fruit cocktail. "We're in Vietnam, sir," he said. "Can't say we like it too much."

Lieutenant Brady nodded. "I hear you," he said, and lit a cigarette. He looked around. "Not much of a hole here, guys."

"Only thing it has to protect tonight is rucks," Michael said. He *really* didn't feel like doing any more digging. Kind of a waste of already limited energy. If other guys got moved to cover these positions tonight, let *them* do the rest of the digging. Seemed only fair.

Lieutenant Brady looked around at the other holes nearby, then nodded.

"We staying here tomorrow, L-T?" Snoopy asked. "Since we got the mortars dug in so deep and all?"

Lieutenant Brady shrugged. "Hard to say, Snoopy. We're still waiting for the word from HQ."

Okay, that was honest. Michael had no problem with honesty. He sipped his 7-Up.

"How your feet doing, Snoopy?" Lieutenant Brady asked.

Snoopy made a face. "Pretty nasty."

Lieutenant Brady nodded. "Well, I've ordered new socks and foot powder on the next resupply, so that should help." He looked at Michael. "How's your stomach today?"

Pretty nasty, actually. "Okay," Michael said, and sipped some soda. Nice of him to ask, though.

"Good," Lieutenant Brady said, and Michael got the feeling that he actually did care about the answers people gave to his questions. About how the two of them felt. Not, in Michael's experience, like an officer at all. "Remember," he said, "either of you has a problem around here, you come straight to me, okay? I'll handle it from there." Then, he looked at Michael.

Ah. Sounded like Kendrick was bitching and moaning around the CP. Funny how that didn't surprise him a bit. Michael sighed, taking out a cigarette of his own. Scary how fast something you'd never done in your life could become a habit. "I didn't start it, sir," he said quietly.

"That isn't really the point, is it?" Lieutenant Brady asked. "We're all on the same side here. We have to work together."

Hmmm. He was starting to sound a little like an officer now.

"I know the rules are different out here in the

bush," Lieutenant Brady said, "but we can't have anarchy. So — let's stop it before it starts."

In other words, put up *and* shut up. Michael nodded.

Lieutenant Brady nodded, too, and pulled in on his cigarette. The sun was starting to go down, and the jungle, and the other hills below them, looked very dark green. Kind of pretty, actually. Lush. Well, no wonder, with all the damned rain.

"You know," Lieutenant Brady said, "we were at the Point together. He's not such a bad guy."

Hmmm. Hard to imagine Kendrick as an old school buddy. Someone with whom you wanted to stay in touch. Then again, it was also hard to imagine going to West Point. By choice.

"Hell of a ballplayer, too," Lieutenant Brady said.

Oh, yeah. A real *team* player, Michael was guessing. Not that he was one to talk — but, he wasn't going around, pretending to be a leader, either. An example for others.

"What kind of ball?" Snoopy asked. "Uh, sir?"

"*Any* kind of ball. Linebacker, Ping-Pong, pool — you name it." He put out his cigarette, automatically buried it, and then straightened up, arching his back a little. "Anyway. You two be careful out there tonight, okay? Keep your eyes open."

They both nodded, and Lieutenant Brady nodded back, then wandered on towards the next hole.

"*That's* how you get people to do what you want," Michael said. "Treat them with respect."

"Yeah, I guess," Snoopy said, "but scaring the shit out of them works pretty good, too."

Well — yeah. Michael laughed, and swallowed the end of his soda. It would be dark soon, and they would be pulling out. Everything in Vietnam was terrible — but night ambushes just might take first prize. Far as he was concerned, anyway.

They sat there, watching the sun go down. Didn't seem to be much to do, but sit, and worry, and be scared.

"Can we read your letter again?" Snoopy asked.

"Absolutely," Michael said, and reached for his rucksack.

By the time it was dark, and they were ready to head out, it was raining. Naturally. Just hard enough to be unpleasant. They were all wearing their ponchos, and carrying ammo, frags, claymores, flares, and canteens. Thumper and Bear were joining their squad for the night, which meant that there would be eight of them. Bear carried the M-60 for Two Squad, but for this ambush, he was using someone's M-16, because Viper handled the M-60 for 1st Squad, and they didn't need two. Since the M-60 — better known as the pig — weighed about twenty-five pounds — three times as much as a loaded M-16 — Bear was probably pretty happy about this.

If it was possible to be happy while going out on night ambush, in a tiny group, all alone, in the middle of the pitch-black jungle, in Vietnam.

Sergeant Hanson went around checking everyone, to make sure they were carrying the right stuff, and would be carrying it quietly. Once they set out from the NDP, complete noise and light discipline would be in effect. Michael had heard people say that sometimes patrols faked going out on ambush — just called in the coordinates and hourly sit-reps to HQ, who didn't know the difference, one way or the other, but obviously, that wasn't Sergeant Hanson's style. And, even if it was, the Company CO, Captain Frazier, probably wouldn't go for it. Michael hadn't actually met him — just seen a stocky, fortyish man with a stiff, graying brush cut, walking around forcefully — but word had it, the guy *wished* his troops would give him a nickname like Blood'n'Guts. Michael kind of hoped *not* to meet him — he had a feeling — call it an intuition, even — that they weren't going to hit it off real well. For one thing, Frazier looked too much like his high school football coach. Who was a jerk. At least, his brother Dennis had had sense enough not to go out for football. With luck, he would have sense enough to stay out of the Army, too. Canada, college — whatever it took.

"*Meat,*" Sergeant Hanson said, in a voice that indicated he had probably tried to get his attention more than once.

Quickly, Michael looked up. It was so dark now that it was hard to see him at all.

"Meat, I want you to — "

Oh, shit, he wasn't going to have to walk point, was he? For the first time? In the *dark*?

" — walk slack," Sergeant Hanson said.

Okay. Good. The slack guy walked right behind the point guy, covering him, and watching the jungle, so that the point guy could concentrate on looking for trails and booby traps and all. In some patrols, the slack guy carried a compass, too, made sure they stayed on course, but he was guessing Sergeant Hanson would want to handle that.

"You step where I step, okay?" Sergeant Hanson said.

Michael nodded. If he could *see* where he stepped.

They were all lined up now, and they moved out through the perimeter, Sergeant Hanson in the lead. Technically, squad leaders were never supposed to walk point — because the odds of getting killed were too high, Michael figured — but, it was a rule that seemed to get broken a lot.

They were going down the hill to a stream about 2500 meters away. There was, apparently, a place where two trails met up near the stream, and it was presumed that the enemy might just come diddy-bopping along, without a care in the world, not expecting an ambush in such a completely obvious place. Seemed doubtful, but since Michael would *prefer* to not run into the enemy, he wasn't about to argue with the logic.

Actually, it would be sort of funny if, because it *was* such an obvious place, the VC set up an ambush there too. Great minds thinking alike, and all. Then, they could all stand around together and be perplexed by this amazing coincidence. Laugh a lot, share some brews, exchange addresses.

Not likely.

It was a long rainy walk, over rough ground, and he could feel his legs trembling with almost every step. Thank God it was dark, so none of the others could see how nervous he was. But — this was scary. This was dangerous. Even though it was raining — pouring, really — he was still sweating up a storm. They all stayed very close together, counting off in whispers every so often to make sure everyone was still there. That no one had gotten separated. Lost.

He *really*, really, really hoped they didn't run into anything tonight. Any*one*.

Sergeant Hanson stopped a couple of times — checking the compass? — then moved on, and since they had to be quiet, Michael couldn't ask why. He wasn't sure he wanted to know, anyway. He was scared enough as it was.

He could hear the stream well before they got to it, and then felt the ground change under his feet as they moved onto a well-packed, if muddy, trail. The trail crossed another, right near the stream, and Sergeant Hanson set up four guys along the side of each of them. The ambush was sort of like an L, but a very short one. Michael was going to be with Finnegan this time, and Snoopy was next to them, with Viper, so he could feed the .60 if they needed it.

They set up their claymores so they would explode up and across the trails, and Finnegan and Thumper set up trip flares too, a ways up each trail. Before leaving the NDP, he and Finnegan had agreed that Michael would take the first watch. They would be switching off every two hours.

Creeping out to set up the claymore had been scary as hell. Even though the others were just a few meters away, he'd felt very vulnerable. Very alone. Unraveling the wire back to his position, connecting it to the detonator, making sure the safety was on. Making sure the safety *worked*. Laying out some grenades, where he could get to them easily. Quickly. Checking his gun. Checking everything. Then, it was time to wait. And watch. And wait. And get wet. Very wet.

A little after three — oh, all *right*, 0300; why the Army couldn't just use normal time, like everyone else, he didn't know — the rain finally stopped. So, all Michael could hear was the stream, and dripping. Lots of dripping, all around him. All *over* him. He was sitting in the mud, with his boots buried above the ankle. Very unpleasant.

He knew there were leeches on him, but he

was so wet, he couldn't really feel where. As long
as they stayed off his face — and out of his
crotch — he decided not to worry about it. He
checked both places, and couldn't feel anything,
but he put extra bug juice on his neck, and where
his pants met his boots. Discourage them a little,
maybe. And — he had to stop thinking about
them, and wondering where on his body they
were. Mosquitoes, at least, he could *feel*.

Not that that was much fun, either.

He could smell bug juice. He could smell wet
rotting jungle vegetation. He could smell Finnegan. Or maybe it was just himself — it was
hard to tell. He could hear the water. He could
hear a little bit of wind. He could hear his heart
beating. At one point, miles and miles away, he
could hear some artillery. That was it. He had
to keep blinking — hard — and biting the inside
of his cheek — very hard — to stay awake.

Then, he smelled something else, and sat up
straighter. Something — what the hell was it? He
could have sworn it was — fish. In the stream,
maybe? Except it wasn't like you could smell fish
swimming. He didn't think. Besides, this fish
smelled rotten. Old. Had a dead fish washed up
on the bank, maybe, or was he just losing his
mind? Because, he could really swear that he —

a noise! A little rustle, off to his left. And everyone in the squad was off to his *right*.

There was someone out there. There really was. Oh, Christ. Did he wait for them to come closer, or — there *was* someone out there. An animal, carrying a dead fish? No, an animal wouldn't be that quiet, only a person would try to — he reached for one of his grenades, glad that he had straightened the pins in advance. That it was ready to go.

But — what if he threw it, and he was wrong and just gave away their position? Or — what if there were a whole lot of them out there, and the squad got over-run because he made a mistake. Didn't wait long enough, or waited too long, or didn't blow the claymore at the right time, or — he *smelled* fish. He did. And it was getting stronger.

Do it. Take some initiative. Better to do something, than nothing. Just as he was drawing his arm back, grenade clenched in his fist, a trip flare went off, and he armed the grenade, then threw it as hard as he could in that direction. As it went off, he blew one of the claymores too, almost sure that he could see shadowy running figures in the eerie light from the flare. Almost.

Before he could decide if he had made a mistake or not, there was a whole lot of shooting, red *and* green tracers slicing wildly through the air, which meant that they really were out there. He'd never actually seen it before, but he knew that Viet Cong weapons fired green tracers. American weapons fired red. Anyway — they were everywhere, like Christmas lights gone berserk, all flying above his head.

Other claymores were going off, people were yelling and shooting, and Michael pressed into the mud as hard as he could, as low as he could, trying to cover his head with his arm. Protect himself. He slammed a fresh magazine into his gun, then fired back at the green tracers. Tried to, anyway. Even with all of the noise, he could hear himself gasping for breath, too scared to shout, and next to him, Finnegan was panting too, both of them shooting like crazy, running through several magazines of twenty rounds each.

Then, for no apparent reason, all of the shooting and yelling stopped, and there was a silence that seemed to last an hour, but probably lasted for only a second or two. Someone — Sergeant Hanson? — shot off a flare and in the sudden light, Michael couldn't see anything but jungle. No people. If they had ever been there — they had, right? — they were gone now. He thought.

He hoped. Only — now what were they supposed to do? Christ, he was scared. It was so *dark*.

He reached over to touch Finnegan's arm, lightly.

"I don't know," Finnegan whispered.

That made two of them. Michael's hands were shaking so much that it was hard to yank another magazine out of the bandolier across his chest and reload his gun — but he sure as hell wasn't going to lie here with it *unloaded*. His breath was coming out in quick bursts, and he gulped a few times, fighting the urge to jump up and run away screaming. But — he had to be quiet. To stay still.

"Anyone hit?" a low voice asked. Sergeant Hanson.

There were several whispered "No"s. Thank God.

"Hold your positions," Sergeant Hanson said, even lower.

An order. Good. Something tangible to do. Michael gulped, and gripped his machine gun so tightly that his hands cramped. His throat hurt. His stomach hurt. He was wet. He was cold. He was fucking terrified. He wanted a cigarette. He wanted to go to the bathroom. He wanted to cry. He wanted to go home.

Also — weird as hell — he really wanted something to eat. Candy, maybe. A Milky Way. Or — oh, Christ — *potato chips*. He really wanted some potato chips.

Someone — Hanson? Jankowski? — was whispering coordinates into the radio, and when the first marking round came in, Michael flinched. Gulped. Almost screamed. Then, he felt Finnegan's hand, patting him on the back, and he gulped again, trying to stay cool. Brave. To stop shaking.

More whispering, then another white phosphorus round. Then, real rounds — HEs — walking away from them, in the direction the VC must have gone. They *had* been there, right? The ground shook when each artillery round hit, and Michael shook even more. Finnegan kept his hand on his back, reaching up to give his shoulder a hard, comforting squeeze. Michael was embarrassed that someone else knew he was so scared — but prayed that he wouldn't take his hand off, either. Wouldn't let go of him. Leave him alone.

A couple of gunships came in next, spraying hell out of the area down the trail, more red tracers sweeping to the ground, and then, they were gone. And it was very, very quiet.

For lack of a better idea, Michael let out his

breath. Relaxed a little. Finnegan's hand gave his shoulder another squeeze, then withdrew.

"Thanks," Michael whispered, although he was still pretty damned embarrassed.

"Don't sweat it," Finnegan whispered back, and they stayed on the ground, silently, waiting for first light.

CHAPTER 6

JUST BEFORE DAWN, Sergeant Hanson crept down the trail, motioning for Thumper to come with him, and for the rest of them to stay put — and stay on guard. It was drizzling a little, and there was ground fog everywhere — even over the stream. Spooky.

When they came back down the trail, they both looked frustrated, and Sergeant Hanson was carrying a battered AK-47 by the stock. Michael figured that that meant no bodies, and probably no indication that all the firepower had had any effect at all. Sergeant Hanson whispered something to Jankowski, who nodded, and broke squelch on the radio, whispering something into it.

Then, Sergeant Hanson gestured for Finnegan to move out one way, and Thumper to move out the other way, tapping his ear to indicate that he wanted them to act as Listening Posts. He motioned for the rest of them to stay on guard, and he went out to make sure that all of their claymores had been blown, and that there were none to collect. One was still there, and he retrieved it, coiling the wire as he came back.

Finnegan and Thumper silently returned, each making an "OK" motion with one hand, and Sergeant Hanson nodded, then motioned for everyone to fall in. They all took the same positions in line they had had the night before, and then, they moved out.

Sergeant Hanson set a slow and deliberate pace, keeping them well off any trails, and Michael tried to concentrate on both the jungle around them, and everything Sergeant Hanson did. Concentrate on not being afraid. Yeah, right. Point. Christ. He couldn't imagine being able to do it himself. He should never, ever have said yes.

They were so hyper-alert and tense that when some damned bird came bursting out of some brush to the right, almost all of them hit the dirt, scrambling towards whatever cover they could find. In Michael's case, a not terribly thick tree root. The bird flew away and none of them made a sound, slowly, cautiously, getting up and moving on.

By the time they got back to the NDP, it was

almost 0800, and Michael, personally, was a wreck. As a result, the atmosphere at the NDP seemed almost — festive. Guys eating breakfast, filling sandbags, sleeping inside their foxholes. Only about half the company was there, indicating that everyone else was out pulling guard, or that they really *were* spending the day here, and squads had been sent out on patrols. 0800 was kind of late for them to break camp and move on, but — it was the Army, so who the hell knew. Logic was not to be expected.

"Assemble in our sector," Sergeant Hanson said, quietly, once they were inside the perimeter, and all standing there, tightly gripping their weapons. "Fifteen mikes." Mikes, being minutes.

It was the first time any of them had spoken, and the rest of them all nodded, and headed towards their foxholes.

"You guys hit some shit last night, hunh?" a shaggily mustached guy, who was shaving out of a couple of inches of water inside his helmet, said as they walked by.

"It was about a whole *battalion*," Snoopy said. "But they were real scared of us, and they ran away, fast as can be."

This broke the tension, which was a relief. Michael let his M-16 fall to his side, checking to make sure it was on safety, then taking his hand off the selector switch.

"Any action here?" Jankowski asked, easing the radio off his shoulders, then shrugging to try and loosen the stiff muscles in his neck.

The guy shrugged, using a knife to very carefully trim a few mustache hairs. His first mustache, no question. "They was probin' 3rd Platoon, seemed like," he said, "but we didn't find nothing."

So what else was new.

Another guy came over, toothbrush hanging out of his mouth, shirtless, and wearing several thick strands of ornate wooden beads. "You boys git some?" he asked.

They all looked at Thumper, who shrugged.

"Found some shell casings," he said. "Some blood." Then, he shrugged again. "Same old, same old."

Viper shook his head, draping the M-60 over his shoulder. "Later," he said, and headed for his foxhole.

"We staying here today, or what?" Snoopy asked.

The guy with the beads spit a mouthful of toothpaste onto the ground. "The word at stand-to was, they're gonna lift us outta here, tomorrow."

"*Lift?*" Jankowski said. "No walking?"

Both of the guys nodded.

"Oh, *yes*," Finnegan said.

"We got some slack today," the guy with the mustache said, squinting into a small piece of mirror, then cutting another stray hair. "Digging and patrols, is all."

"The Grunt God is smiling on us," Thumper said, and bumped fists with a very willing Snoopy.

"Lifting us where?" Michael asked. If it was going to be a combat assault or something, it might be kind of early to start celebrating.

"Dunno," Bead-Boy said. If that wasn't his nickname — it probably should be. "Smitty heard we got a new AO." AO, being Area of Operations.

"The beach, man," Thumper said. "Tell me we got the beach."

Michael perked up at that thought. The beach. *That'd* be all right.

"I dunno," the guy said. "Smitty heard Que Son Valley."

"Is that good or bad?" Bear asked, looking uneasy.

Sounded pretty ominous to Michael, too.

"2nd NVA." The guy spit some more toothpaste. "It sucks."

Real ominous. On that happy note. Michael followed the others towards their sector.

Before anyone had time to open some C-rats or take a leak or anything, Sergeant Hanson had already appeared to brief them.

"Okay, guys, listen up," he said, sounding more tired than he looked. Somehow, even when he was as muddy and unshaven as everyone else, he still seemed — alert. Damn near perky. If you could use the word perky, for a guy that big. "Get something to eat, get your weapons and your holes squared away, then grab a couple hours' sleep. We're on ambush again tonight, and we're going to move out at 1600."

"Are we getting lifted out of here tomorrow?" Snoopy asked.

Sergeant Hanson nodded. "Yeah, that's the word right now. We're going to a new firebase. Alpha Company's already there, with the engineers, and starting tomorrow, we'll be helping them dig in. The rest of the battalion's going to be coming in, too, over the next few days."

"Crush says we've got a new AO?" Jankowski said.

"Looks that way," Sergeant Hanson said. "The rest of the brigade's going straight to Tam Ky, to take over for the 101st Airborne. The 198th's taking our place at Chu Lai. From there — I don't know. Anyway, get yourselves something to eat, then get to work. Make sure you clean your ammo too." As they started to drift off, he pointed at Michael and Finnegan, indicating for them to stay behind. "Which one of you was on guard last night?" he asked.

Oh, hell, he *knew* he'd screwed up — somehow. Damn. "Me," Michael said.

"Unh-hunh," Sergeant Hanson said, and studied him. "You react that fast to the flare, or you see them first?"

Michael frowned. He hadn't exactly *seen* them. "I, uh — " Would they think he was losing his mind? "It's weird, Sarge, but — I smelled *fish*."

Sergeant Hanson nodded. "Nuoc-mam."

What? Michael frowned again.

"Fish sauce," Sergeant Hanson said. "They eat it on just about everything. The wind's right, we can smell it on them, the same way they can smell meat on us. Cigarettes, deodorant, after-shave — any damn thing like that. The more you smell like the jungle," he looked down wryly at himself, his fatigues torn and filthy, "the better." Then, he looked up. "Here, however, is where you fucked up. If they're out there, don't keep it to yourself. Wake up your buddy, so he can pass it down the line."

Okay. That made sense. Good sense. Michael nodded.

"Once they trip the flare, yeah, you pretty much have to react," Sergeant Hanson said, "but normally, you want to wait until you're sure they're in range, and you have an idea of how many you're dealing with. I'm guessing that was just a small patrol last night, but you never know. If it had just been the point element, we could have had a whole damned company on top of us."

Michael nodded.

"But, yeah," Sergeant Hanson said. "You go with your frags first, then your claymores, so you don't give away our position. Muzzle flashes, tracers."

Michael nodded, still not quite sure if he was getting criticized, or praised. Judging from Sergeant Hanson's expression, and the way his arms were folded, he hadn't decided, either.

"You've got good instincts for a boot, kid," Sergeant Hanson said, finally. "Keep using them." Then, he tapped one of the frags hanging from his web gear. "We're inside the perimeter now, guys — bend those pins." He smiled at them. When he smiled, he suddenly looked his age. "And get some breakfast, too, okay?"

Right. As Sergeant Hanson went back towards

the CP, Michael bent the pins on his remaining frags, then looked at Finnegan. "So — I did the right thing?" he asked, just to be sure.

Finnegan nodded. "B-plus, A-minus."

Could be worse. Then again, in Vietnam, there wasn't much room for error. You were right, you were lucky, or you were dead. So — he'd have to do better.

Then, remembering something else, he flushed slightly. "Um, last night," he said, too embarrassed to elaborate.

"Last night was scary as shit," Finnegan said.

"Yeah, but — " Michael stopped. "You were scared too?"

Finnegan tilted his boonie hat up enough to look at him, his face so muddy and filthy that his eyes looked even more blue than usual. They also looked miserable. "I'm scared of *everything* here," he said. "Half the time, I can't even move I'm so scared. J.D. kept me going, man. And now — " He shivered. "I only got four months in, Meat, and I *know* I'm going home in a bag."

Damn. He should think occasionally, before he said things. Michael sighed. "I'm sorry, man. I should just — shut up, is what I should do."

Finnegan shrugged and they stood there, awkwardly.

"I think I smell turkey loaf," Michael said.

Finnegan sniffed the air, looked over in Snoopy's direction, then smiled a little. "I think you do, too," he said.

Christ, he was tired. Too tired to sleep, even. He didn't feel like eating, he didn't feel like cleaning and oiling his gun, and he *really* didn't feel like digging. He sat down on a wet sandbag, the smell of scorched turkey loaf doing nothing to increase his enthusiasm.

"Hey, there, soldier," Snoopy said.

Michael nodded, deciding that the only thing he could stomach was some peanut butter, jelly, and crackers. He wasn't a big jelly fan, but the peanut butter was dry as hell, and the jelly made it taste a little better. Not much.

"*You* look happy," Snoopy said.

Michael nodded. "Never better." At least the rain had pretty much stopped. His hands were incredibly filthy — worse than he'd ever seen them — and he'd spent a lot of time underneath car hoods in his life. When his father got home from work, he would spend about twenty minutes inside the downstairs bathroom, scrubbing and scrubbing his hands, working with a sturdy nailbrush. Even so, he usually couldn't get all of the motor oil and grease out, and when he was dressed up — at church, or wherever — Michael had often noticed him keeping his hands self-consciously in his pockets.

Doc came over with malaria pills. "Here you go, kids."

Snoopy put his on top of a spoonful of turkey loaf, then ate it.

Michael just looked at his pill, feeling very, very tired.

"Come on," Doc said impatiently. "I got things to do, kid."

Right. "Sure, kid," Michael said, and reached over for Snoopy's canteen cup, swallowing the pill with a mouthful of tepid, extremely sweet coffee. He made a face, and handed it back.

"You're welcome," Snoopy said.

"Unh-hunh," Michael said, eating a fingerful of plain peanut butter to try and kill the sugar taste. Didn't help much.

Doc checked their names off on his limp, ragged list. "Take your boots off today, kids," he said. "Dry out. Long as you can." Then, he looked around. "Yo! Finnegan! Hold it right there!" he said, and hustled over with his pills.

Michael watched him go. "Does he ever get tired?"

"Nope," Snoopy said. "The only doc I ever seen does all his own humping and digging too."

Not surprising, somehow. Too tired to finish his breakfast, Michael decided to get some of his own digging out of the way. Since it was someone's old position that had been caved in, the dirt was loose — if heavy, from the rain. If he made it through his tour in this damned place, he was either going to go home brawny as hell — or with a very bad back.

Snoopy looked down at his unfinished turkey loaf. "Do I have to help?" he asked.

Michael shook his head, digging. They had done enough work the night before so that it didn't take long, but he had to stop a few times to bail some of the water out of the hole with his helmet, setting aside his plastic liner, where he stored his cigarettes and toilet paper, first. They were all still relatively dry. Amazing. Everything else of his was completely soaked. He dug a couple of grenade sumps — in case that son-of-a-bitch Kendrick came by — and made them extra deep. That way, if it rained some more, the water might drain into the holes, and stay *off* them.

"That's good, man," Snoopy said, eating a cookie from the B-2 unit in his C-ration. The B-2 unit had all the little extras in it, aside from the main meal. "Looks good."

"Glad you like it," Michael said. He filled a

sandbag with mud, then stacked it on the very small wall they had built the night before. He would do five, and then quit. "It'll look even better when *you* do a bunch more of these bags," he said.

Snoopy nodded, taking his time with his cookie.

Michael filled and stacked six bags — one extra, to be a sport — then, sat down in the mud, leaning against the wall to clean his gun, getting his little kit out of his very wet rucksack. He didn't have his towel anymore — it had gotten ruined when he used it to clean up Finnegan after J.D. — except, he wasn't going to think about that. Get his stomach going again. Point was, he usually liked to break down his M-16, then spread the pieces out on his towel, so they wouldn't get lost. All the pins were so small, it was easy as hell to drop them — and hard as hell to find them, so he stuck them between his teeth, while he cleaned and oiled everything else. Tasted just great.

They all oiled their guns every chance they got, and completely cleaned and disassembled them once or twice a day, too. The stupid things were famous for jamming. He'd heard AK-47s were a lot better, which didn't seem fair. Both sides should have the same quality guns, for Christ's sakes. On the other hand, *his* side had air power, and theirs didn't.

He had no guilt whatsoever about this.

When he was finished reassembling his gun, he leaned it next to him, and got to work on his ammo. It *was* pretty muddy. He looked up at Snoopy, who was filling sandbags without much energy.

"Got any tape?" he asked. If you taped two magazines back to back, you could just flip it over and have fresh ammo instantly, instead of digging around for another magazine in the heat of the moment. Saved time. Always a good idea when someone was shooting at you. J.D. had taught him that.

And look where it had gotten him. Except, of course, he wasn't going to think about that. No way.

"Nope," Snoopy said, digging.

"Shouldn't we tape our magazines together?" Michael asked.

"Yep," Snoopy said, spilling more mud than he managed to drop into the open sandbag he was holding. He tried again, but the mud slipped off his entrenching tool before he even lifted it all of the way off the ground.

Michael watched him. "That's going to take you all day."

Snoopy nodded sadly. "Yep."

Right. Michael sighed, and got up, taking the entrenching tool from him. "Hold the damned bag open."

"You already did your share," Snoopy said.

Michael sighed again. "Just do it."

"Well — if you *want* to help," Snoopy said, cheerfully, and held a bag open.

"I want to very much," Michael said, grimly, and got to work.

CHAPTER 7

THEY GOT the job done pretty quickly, even setting up a few sticks — driving them into the mud, so about a foot and a half was still above ground — and attaching their ponchos to them, so that they would have some little shade shelters. Or rain shelters, as the case might be.

"A couple guys work together, they can just do it lickety-split," Snoopy said. Cheerfully.

"Unh-hunh," Michael said, and sat down to attend to his ammo. And check the pins on his frags again, while he was at it. "You bend back your frag pins?"

"Nope," Snoopy said, pouring some water into his empty turkey loaf can, then dropping a couple of heat tabs into his stove and lighting them, so he could heat the water up.

Oh. "Are you going to?" Michael asked.

"Maybe," Snoopy said, holding the can by the bent-back lid, over the stove.

Maybe. Great. "You really should," Michael said. "It's much safer."

Snoopy nodded, making cocoa with extra cream substitute and sugar, stirring it with a small stick.

"Come on," Michael said, uneasily. He was, before his very own eyes, becoming living proof that a little knowledge was a dangerous thing. But — no knowledge was more dangerous. "Just do it, okay?"

"You're a very *nervy* little cherry, is what *I* think," Snoopy said, stirring his cocoa. Heat tabs took a lot longer than C-4. On the other hand, C-4 generally had more important uses.

"I don't think there's anything wrong with being careful," Michael said. Stiffly. J.D. should have, for Christ's sakes, been more careful. Looked where he was going. But if a point guy that good couldn't see an artillery round mine until it was too late, how the hell was *he* going to be able to find them? What were *his* odds of making it out of this place in one piece? Not good. Not good at all. And Snoopy was just going to sit there, jerking around, like they were at Disneyland or someplace. Fine. Swell. He popped bullets out of one of his magazines. Harder than necessary.

Snoopy looked over at him. "Take it easy, man. I had a bad night too, okay?"

Right. Michael gritted his teeth, but then, nodded.

"And tonight, we got to do it again, and this time, they'll probably be there waiting for us," Snoopy said. "So, right now, I'm going to sit here and have something sweet to drink. *Okay?*"

Michael nodded.

"Okay, then." Snoopy took a sip of cocoa, then winced as he burned his mouth. "Ow." Then, he held the can towards Michael. "Want some?"

"Think I'll wait 'til it cools," Michael said.

Snoopy nodded. "Think that's a good idea." He set the can down in the mud, then began fixing the pins on his grenades. When he was done, he looked over. "Happy now?"

"I'm sorry. I didn't mean to be a jerk," Michael said.

"Well — way I figure," Snoopy said, some of his good humor returning, "you probably can't help yourself."

Michael nodded.

"So, have some chocolate," Snoopy said.

Michael nodded, picked up the can, and promptly burned his mouth. Seemed only fair.

And — it amused Snoopy, so that was good. However, his tongue and lip now hurt.

The sun was coming out now — it was starting to get hot — and he took his boots off. He rinsed his socks with a little water from one of his canteens, squeezed them out, then hung them to dry from one of the stick-poles of the poncho shelter. He washed his feet too — they looked disgusting — then, set his helmet down and propped his feet up on top of it to keep them out of the mud. Then, he leaned back against the sandbags to continue cleaning his ammo.

"Your feet are almost as ugly as mine," Snoopy said.

Michael nodded.

Snoopy took his boots off too, went through the same barely effective cleaning ritual, then sat back to drink his cocoa. "Nineteen," he said, as Michael started putting bullets back into one of his magazines.

Michael stopped. "Nineteen what?"

Snoopy shrugged, frowning down at his left heel, where the skin was almost completely peeled away. "Sarge says if you load 'em up full, the springs get lousy, and it'll jam on you."

Michael took out the twentieth bullet. If Sergeant Hanson said that, in fact, Columbus was mistaken, and the earth was very definitely very flat, Michael would probably take his word for it. Stay the hell away from the edge. "How come the Army doesn't tell us stuff like that?" he asked.

" 'Cause they're stupid," Snoopy said.

No argument there. Michael kept cleaning his ammo and reloading his magazines. Not looking up. "Didn't mean to be telling you what to do," he said. "Before."

Snoopy shrugged. "It's cool."

Actually, it wasn't. It was rude. "I, uh, this is kind of — new, for me," he said, keeping his eyes on the bullets in his lap.

"Hey, I ain't been out here much longer — know what I mean?" Snoopy said.

Michael shook his head. "That's not what I mean. I — " Could he explain it? Did he *want* to explain it? Not really. He shook his head again, snapping bullets back into a magazine.

"You best go on," Snoopy said. " 'Cause I am sure enough on pins and needles."

Michael grinned. "How many sisters do you have?"

"Three." Snoopy grinned, too. "I'm the baby."

Very easy to picture. Especially since he was

sitting there with a hot chocolate mustache.

"Gonna get me off my pincushion, or what?" Snoopy asked.

Right. The cocoa smelled good, and Michael reached over to help himself to a sip. Smelled better than it tasted.

"Talk to me," Snoopy said. "I'm a very lonely young man, far away from home."

Right. "I'm just saying I'm sorry," Michael said. "I'm used to being — casual. How you doing, and see you later, and not getting real tight with anyone."

Snoopy frowned. "Yeah, but — you got friends back home, right?"

"I've got — guys I know," Michael said. "Kind of always liked it that way." Kind of. "Or — fuck it, I don't know. Forget it." The hell was wrong with him, talking like this? He kept his eyes down, wondering if his face was as red as it felt.

"I don't know," Snoopy said, twisting to look at the seat of his pants. "There are still many, many needles here, that hurt a whole lot."

Michael pressed his teeth together. "So I'm sorry if I don't treat you right, okay? I'm not good at it."

"Well, I know that," Snoopy said. "Besides, you're not always a jerk. Just mostly."

Right. Michael went back to his ammo.

" 'Sides," Snoopy said. "Who says I *want* to be your buddy?"

Good point.

"Feel sorry for you, is all," Snoopy said.

"Likewise," Michael said.

It was quiet for a minute, as Snoopy drained his can of cocoa, then broke down his M-16 to start cleaning it.

"Wouldn't trust a white boy who was real friendly, right off, anyway," he said, suddenly.

Michael frowned over at him. "What does *that* have to do with it?"

"Lots, far as I'm concerned," Snoopy said. "I'll take a grouch like you over fake-friendly, anytime."

Michael kept frowning, not quite sure how to take that.

" 'Fore the Army, I never really *knew* any white boys," Snoopy said. "Now my life depends on 'em."

Hmmm. Michael couldn't think of a response.

"You know a lot of brothers?" Snoopy asked. "Back in the World?"

No. Michael shook his head.

"Seems like you don't notice, though," Snoopy said. "Like you treat a guy straight." Snoopy grinned. "Even though you are one *very* pathetic cherry."

"Lucky I got *you* around," Michael said. "To teach me how to act."

"You know it," Snoopy said, and started cleaning his ammo, too.

They finished at about the same time, and crawled under the poncho shelter to get some sleep. The shade wasn't nearly as cool as Michael had thought it would be. Hoped it would be. But, he was too tired to worry about it, falling asleep almost before he could fold his flak jacket into some semblance of a pillow. Snoopy, who was using the mud for a pillow, was already asleep.

When he heard shots, he woke up instantly, grabbing for his gun, scrambling barefoot into their foxhole, Snoopy right behind him. They slammed their guns into the firing positions they'd formed with sandbags, and crouched in the hole, ready to defend the perimeter against whatever assault was coming.

"I don't see anything!" Snoopy yelled. "You see anything?"

Michael shook his head, his heart thumping so hard that it actually hurt inside his ears.

"Hold your fire!" someone else was yelling. "Hold your goddamn fire!"

Turned out, some guy in 2nd Platoon had tripped, and his gun went off. Another guy nearby had taken a ricochet in the leg. Hell of a way to wake up. Only, once Doc whacked him up with some morphine, the guy was happy as hell because he had taken the round right through the knee, would probably never walk right again, and that meant he was on his way home. Like they said, a million-dollar wound. The platoon sergeant for 2nd Platoon — an older guy, had to be at least thirty — spent the next ten, fifteen minutes yelling about dumb-ass kids who didn't know enough to keep their safeties on, but no one was really listening, just waiting and watching with a certain amount of envy as the medevac came in, and took the guy away for good.

Michael stood there as the helicopter took off, the guy sitting inside with a big grin, popping a red smoke grenade out the cargo bay, and waving.

"Probably hurts," Snoopy said. "Getting it in the knee."

Michael nodded. Part of him really wouldn't mind finding out. If he had some way of knowing that the injury was going to be relatively minor.

"Lucky son-of-a-bitch," Snoopy said.

Michael nodded.

They watched, as the smoke faded away, and the helicopter flew out of sight.

"Bet he did it on purpose," Snoopy said. "Cooked it up with his buddy."

Which hadn't even occurred to him. Michael looked over. "Really?"

"Hell, yes," Snoopy said. "Happens all the time. Only, mostly, people shoot themselves in the foot."

Didn't exactly sound like the worst idea he had ever heard. Michael looked down, noticing that he didn't have his boots on. Neither did Snoopy. Their feet *did* look terrible.

"Could've been an accident," Snoopy said, but he didn't sound convinced.

Michael nodded. He wasn't all that convinced, either. Now that he gave it some thought. His socks were pretty much dry, and he rewashed his feet, then sat down to put the socks back on. Then, he slipped on his boots, leaving them unlaced.

"And — you could really hurt yourself," Snoopy said, putting his socks and boots back on, too.

Michael nodded.

"Kind of chicken-shit," Snoopy said. "When you think about it."

Michael nodded.

"*I'd* never do it," Snoopy said. Uncertainly.

"Me, neither," Michael said.

They looked at each other, looked away, and crawled back under their poncho shelter to get some more sleep.

CHAPTER 8

THE AMBUSH that night was quiet. Thank God. It was also long, and dark, and rainy. When they got back to the NDP, wet and tired, everyone else was either pulling guard, or caving in their foxholes. Waste, to go to all that work, then just take it apart.

The largest group of guys pulling guard was spread out around the LZ. Only, now it was, Michael supposed, a PZ. As in, Pick-up Zone. They were going to be lifted out, one platoon at a time, five or six guys on each chopper, starting at 0900. The last platoon to leave would stay behind a little longer, to police the area.

"Viper, Meat, Thumper — pull perimeter," Sergeant Hanson said, back from reporting in at the CP. "The rest of you, fill in those holes. Switch off every half hour. 1st Platoon pulls out after 3rd and Weapons."

Good. That meant 2nd Platoon would be

stuck policing the area. Which, mainly, would be burying all the C-ration cans, empty ammo cans, and everything else people had discarded out of fatigue, stupidity, or just plain laziness. They didn't want to leave anything behind for the VC to find — and, more importantly, *use*.

There wasn't enough time to stop and eat, and considering how nervous Michael was about getting on a helicopter to go God only knew where, it was probably just as well. Everyone else just seemed glad that they weren't going to have to do any walking today.

The slicks — general transport helicopters, known more formally as Hueys, or UH-1s — came in, in groups of four or five. One would touch down, a squad would scramble aboard, and the next one would land almost before the other one had had time to take off. It was all very swift and efficient, with gunships cruising around in the sky, above the formation of slicks, just in case the VC got any bright ideas.

It was kind of awesome, really, and if Michael hadn't been so nervous when it was 1st Squad's turn to jump aboard, he probably would have given it even more thought. Talk about the American war machine. If he were a Viet Cong soldier, looking up at the crowded sky, he would pretty much decide to call it quits, right then and there. All that firepower and technology made you wonder why the United States hadn't already *won* this damned war.

His particular chopper took off before he could get all the way aboard — it was hard as hell to jump up in the air, while carrying sixty or seventy pounds on your back — and Finnegan and Jankowski had to haul him inside. The slick lifted off at such a steep angle that he wanted to press into the metal flooring as hard as he could, and pray not to fall out, but he would look stupid, so instead, he moved until he was sort of wedged in behind the door-gunner. *Well* behind the door-gunner.

Snoopy, sitting next to him, gave him a big grin and a thumbs-up, which Michael returned. Weakly. And, even over the noise of the chopper, Michael could hear him laughing. At least it was cooler, once they were up in the air. Breezy. Rather pleasant, really. As long as he didn't think about how high they were, and how fast they were swooping along.

They flew over the jungle hills, then over some lowlands. Little villages. Lots of rice paddies. From up above, it looked like the paddies were all on different levels — like some crazed set of checkerboard stairs. Probably some kind of illusion. They were flying towards more hills and mountains, up above the valley.

Michael could see where they were going well before they landed — a hill with a red spot of bald earth on top, surrounded by thick jungle. It was more of an oval than a circle, heavy equipment spread out haphazardly in the dirt. He had never even been on a firebase and, apparently, he was going to see this one get literally built from the ground up.

The chopper landed, they all jumped off, and then it was gone. Sergeant Hanson motioned for them to follow him, off the landing zone, all of them staying low, Michael holding onto his helmet with one hand as the force of the rotor blades above almost blew it off.

There was a hell of a lot of activity going on all over the hilltop. Guys were everywhere, digging, especially around the battery of 105mm howitzer guns. Howitzers were the most important artillery support for the infantry — and so, they were also the best target for the enemy. As a result, getting them dug in and protected was the top priority. There were six of them, and since Alpha Company had already been working on this firebase for a couple of days, they had made pretty good progress.

The idea was to build huge sandbag walls — parapets — about as thick as they were tall, to surround each gun. The guns were huge — it took at least a five-man team to fire each one — and they needed to have enough room inside the retaining walls to move the guns around, so they could face in the direction a particular fire mission required.

Not that Michael was the world's expert, but he knew that the request for a fire mission would come into the Fire Directional Center — the FDC was either next to, or part of, the Command Post, in the middle of the compound — and it would be relayed to the gun crews at each howitzer. The howitzers were grouped around the CP and FDC in a rough kind of circle. The guy in charge of the gun crew would receive the coordinates of the fire mission, and he would start checking and double-checking, while two other guys set the gun — using aiming stakes and all — at the right angle and elevation, and the other two guys got out the right kind of artillery shell — HE, illumination, whatever, a fuze to screw on the end of it, and however many powder charges it would take to send the shell as far as it needed to go. The shells weighed damn near a hundred pounds, and they would stuff it into the breech tube of the gun, stuff the powder charges in after it, and then, close the gun. The section chief — the guy in charge of the crew — would check and make sure everything was exactly right, and then, the crew would pull the little lanyard that fired the gun, and off it would go. And, all of this would only take a couple of minutes. Tops.

The guns were incredibly noisy — artillery guys were always half deaf after a while — and Michael was pretty sure he would hate firing them almost as much as he hated being a grunt. Well — sort of sure.

Anyway, the key thing for any firebase was to get the big guns dug in. The sandbag walls not only had to be able to protect the gun from getting hit by an enemy mortar, but they also had to protect the rest of the firebase in case it *did* get hit, and the shells exploded. Not a thing Michael ever wanted to witness.

So, a lot of guys were working on the guns, and more guys were building the huge thick bunker that would serve as the FDC. It already had a roof, with a few radio aerials sticking out of it. Next to it, guys were building another big bunker, which Michael guessed was going to be CP living quarters, of some kind.

Other guys were setting little fires, to burn away jungle growth around the area, and clear the ground faster, and Michael could hear explosions down the hill a ways. Probably the engineers, blowing up trees. He had this image of a bunch of guys standing around in railroad hats, but actually, engineers were just the guys who blew up and cleared large areas of jungle, so camps and roads and everything could be built. They would use a lot of plastic explosives, and also wrap detonation cord around groups of trees, and blow them up all at once. Ka-boom! — and what was jungle one minute, was splinters the next.

Easier than using a few tired grunts with small dull machetes.

There were two bulldozers steaming around one end of the perimeter, and Michael wasn't sure if they were just clearing the land, or if more big guns — 81mm mortars, probably — were going to be brought in at some point, and that the bulldozers were preparing accordingly. Either way, this was a pretty damned big operation. If he didn't know better, he'd almost think they were trying to win the war or something.

No. Get serious.

"Meat!" Sergeant Hanson said, impatiently.

Michael looked away from the bulldozers. He was really going to have to do better about paying attention. Or else, he was guessing, have Ser-

geant Hanson slug him. The rest of the squad
was moving away from the howitzers, towards
the perimeter, and he followed them, his rucksack slamming heavily into his back with each
trotting step.

"You three," Sergeant Hanson pointed at Michael, Jankowski, and Snoopy, "start digging a
hootch here." He pointed again, at a spot of bare
ground. "Viper, Finnegan, lose your rucks, and
follow me — you're going to help with the
guns."

Michael looked at the dirt, then looked at
Snoopy. "Is a hootch as big as I think it is?"

Snoopy nodded. Glumly.

"Well." Jankowski took off his helmet and
flak jacket, letting them fall next to his rucksack
and the PRC-25 radio he carried for the squad.
"Let's get started."

Right. Michael got out his entrenching tool.
Below them, a good ways down, there were some
guys stretching rolls of concertina wire — thick
wire with little razors attached to it — around
this part of the perimeter. Later, presumably,
there would be flares and claymores and all sorts
of unpleasant surprises for Victor Charlie. In
case he decided to pay them all a visit.

The hill was smoky and noisy, with the explosions going off, and helicopters coming in

nonstop. Sometimes, they delivered troops; other times, it was the bigger Chinook helicopters — CH-47s — with slings of ammo, water trailers, lots of C-rats, sandbags, and other supplies. The Chinook rotors were so powerful that instead of just dust — mud — the wind actually picked up things like rocks and sticks and whirled them around.

Breakfast seemed to have been forgotten — not to Michael's delight — and he hoped that they were going to be allowed to stop for lunch. Digging was tough work. Hot work. *Boring* work.

They dug, and they dug, and they dug. Ultimately, the hootch would be big enough to sleep at least three or four guys comfortably. Deep enough, so they could stand up. They would make thick, sandbag walls, and then, they would have to go down to the jungle and drag back logs — which they would probably have to chop themselves — and heave them up on top of the sandbags to form a roof. Then, more sandbags would cover the logs. The roof was the most crucial part of the hootch, since that was where enemy mortars would hit — he hoped *not*. They had to be strong enough to withstand that possibility.

They dug for about three hours straight, making much less progress than Michael would have hoped. Too many damned rocks and roots in the way. The hole was maybe six feet by eight feet — hard to say, really — and they had gotten a foot down. Maybe.

It was early afternoon, hot as hell, and Jankowski let his shovel fall.

"I gotta eat," he said. "I'm starving."

Michael and Snoopy didn't exactly argue, dropping their entrenching tools too. Instantly.

They all dug through their rucksacks for C-rations, then sat down on a big pile of dirt and sandbags. Michael's hands felt numb and swollen from all of his blisters, and he flexed them a few times, trying to get some of the mobility back. One thing he was learning about the Army was that you could be tired, or sick, or in pain — and you did the job, anyway. You might gripe and groan a little — or even a lot — but you did what had to be done. If he were at home, and had blistered his hands this badly raking leaves, say, or shoveling snow, he would probably have quit, and gone inside the house to lie down. Here, he had to just grit his teeth, and get on with it.

So, he was either building character, or else he had fallen so deep into the group mentality that he was incapable of making any sort of decision for himself.

Tough call.

"Pretty soon, they'll be as ugly as your feet," Snoopy said, noticing his blisters.

There was something to look forward to. Michael reached for his P-38 can opener, which was so small, that he had hung it on the chain with his dog tag. Tag, not tags, because his other tag was attached to the laces of his right boot. That way, in case he had to be identified, he had to hope that either his head *or* his foot got blown off, and not both. If he blew up completely, he would just have to hope that someone else saw it happen, so he would be reported as a KIA, and not an MIA, when they had trouble finding the pieces. Like when — if he didn't, for Christ's sakes, stop thinking about it, he was never going to be able to eat again. So, he picked up pieces of a guy, so what. It was over. He should — deal with it, already.

"Trade my ham and limas for your franks and beans," Snoopy offered.

Nobody, in his right mind, ate ham and lima beans. "Never happen," Michael said, and used the P-38 to open his nice, cold lunch.

Jankowski had spaghetti and meatballs, and looked reasonably happy about it. Michael barely knew him, but he seemed like a nice enough guy — tall, with longish, brownish hair.

Kind of gawky-looking, with a very prominent Adam's apple. Probably had played trumpet in the band in high school. Maybe even clarinet. Except his father would always embarrass him by referring to it as a licorice stick.

His blisters hurt. His blisters hurt a whole lot.

"You know something?" Snoopy said with his mouth full. "Chain gangs don't work as hard as we do. We'd be having more fun in *jail*."

The food'd probably be better, too. And — they'd get more sleep. Probably even have mattresses. Flush toilets. *Showers*.

If they passed a bank anytime soon — he was going to do his best to get caught robbing it.

CHAPTER 9

NOBODY CAME to yell at them, so they took their time eating. And, without a boonie hat, Michael was getting pretty sunburned.

War was hell.

"We're not going to come anywhere *near* to finishing this thing tonight," Snoopy said, looking at the hole.

Jankowski looked tired. "You guys haven't seen anything yet. Few months ago, they had us dig in at this one LZ — for about *two weeks,* we were digging — and then, Battalion HQ decides they want us to go to some other damn hill they like better, and start over. So, we tear the whole place apart, go to the new hill, and do it all over again." He shook his head. "It really sucked."

"Better than walking around getting shot at," Snoopy said.

Jankowski shrugged. "I guess so. But they mortared the shit out of us. One night, we lost about twenty guys."

There was a short silence.

"Well, I know I'll sleep better, knowing that," Michael said.

Jankowski nodded, shoveling in spaghetti and meatballs. His second can.

Michael put his barely touched can of franks and beans down, deciding to drink some water instead. Not only was he getting a bad back, and torn-up hands and feet, but Vietnam was also giving him what felt like a damned ulcer. Would they send him home if he got an ulcer? Probably not, considering you had to have a temperature of 103 or 104, for at least three days running, before they decided to send you back to the rear for treatment. He'd heard stories about guys who'd died of malaria and FUOs — mysterious Fevers of Unknown Origin — because they didn't get to the hospital in time. For an ulcer, he'd probably have to throw up blood for a week straight.

"Oh, fuck it," Jankowski said. "It *is* better than walking around the jungle, sweating your guts out." He gulped down the last of his spaghetti, then took out a cigarette. "So." He lit up.

"How'd they get *you* in this man's army, Meat?"

He was dragged, forced, and ordered. "I got a real nice invitation," Michael said.

"Greetings!" Jankowski said, and laughed. "Think I know the one you mean. Where you from again?"

Coffee. He could really use some coffee. "Right outside Denver," Michael said, taking out the little C-rat can stove Snoopy had made for him, and filling his canteen cup with water. "Anyone else want coffee?"

"Hell, yes," Snoopy said.

Michael nodded, filling the canteen cup all the way. Snoopy rarely seemed to drink anything more than part of a cupful. Just enough, presumably, to be cool. He looked at Jankowski, who shook his head. "Where are *you* from?" he asked, lighting a heat tab.

"Tacoma," Jankowski said.

"That's in Washington, Meat," Snoopy said helpfully.

Michael frowned at him. "Do I look stupid?"

Snoopy laughed, instead of answering.

"You can damn near *walk* to Canada from Tacoma," Michael said — and left it at that.

"Yeah." Jankowski grinned wryly. "Had this dumb idea I was supposed to serve my country."

"Had that idea myself," Michael said, and they both nodded, then both shook their heads.

"I just wanted to learn how to use dangerous weapons," Snoopy said, and laughed, as Michael gave him a shove.

"I tell you one thing," Jankowski said. "I always kind of liked rain, growing up there and all, but — " he looked up at the sky — "I sure hate it now."

Michael looked up, too. It was mostly sunny, but that didn't seem to mean much in Vietnam — it could be pouring any minute now. Any second.

"I should've figured they'd get me," Jankowski said. "Had a decent job, up at this cannery, had a car — things were going okay. Should've known Uncle Sam'd fuck it up."

"What kind of car?" Michael asked. The water was hot and he stirred in the coffee packet from his C-ration, then poured half of it into Snoopy's canteen cup.

"Mustang," Jankowski said. "Needed a lot of bodywork, so I got it pretty cheap. I mean, hell — the thing runs, can't say I care much how it *looks*."

No argument there. Michael nodded. "Those are good cars," he said. "You take care of them, they last a long time."

"You know cars?" Jankowski asked.

Michael nodded. "My father has a gas station."

"That what you're going to do when you get back?" Jankowski asked.

Was it? Was he going to *get* back? Did he want to spend his life under a hood? Michael shrugged, and drank some of his coffee. Sugar. Needed some sugar. Needed plenty. Something other than fake powdered cream would be good, too.

Snoopy laughed again. "He *skis* for a living. Spends his day with little boards on his feet."

Jankowski looked impressed. "They pay you for that?"

"Well — I'm ski patrol," Michael said. "Teach some lessons, make sure the lifts work okay, clean the bathrooms — whatever needs doing. Hell, the cook called in sick one time, and they had me and another guy in there, cooking in the lodge restaurant." They weren't half-bad, actually. Better than the regular guy.

Jankowski looked at Snoopy. "They *pay* him for that?"

"Yeah, really." Snoopy stood up. "Tell you what — here's Meat, teaching skiing." Normally, his walk was very bouncy, but now, he started swaggering around, all shoulders and testosterone, and Michael found it more than a little embarrassing that the walk looked so damn familiar. It would be fair to use the word "uncanny." "Hey, you!" Snoopy said, his voice much deeper and gruffer than usual, staring down at an imaginary skier. "Stupid! Get up!" He stood there, arms folded across his chest, waiting impatiently for the poor skier to struggle up. "You're supposed to *stand* on them — *stupid*." He shook his head in disgust, spit on the ground, and swaggered away.

Then, he came back, grinning. "So?"

"That's, that's funny," Michael said, kind of amused — but not about to admit it. "That's — very funny."

"Yep." Snoopy grinned some more. "I'll tell you what, here's what — this is Meat, asking out a girl." He swaggered around a little, stopped, folded his arms, and stared at an imaginary girl across the way. "Hey, you! With the blonde hair! Get over here!"

Yeah, right. Michael looked at Jankowski, who was laughing almost as hard as Snoopy was. "Enjoying yourself?" he asked.

"Hell, yes," Jankowski said. "This is the best lunch I had in about a *month*."

"Oh, yeah?" Michael stood up. "Okay. This is Snoopy asking a girl out." He held out his hand. "Hat, please."

Snoopy took off his boonie hat. "Don't get any white-boy germs on it."

Right. Michael turned away from them, and put on the boonie hat, letting it fall rakishly to one side. Then, he loosened the laces on his left boot so that it was half falling off, and he pulled a couple of his pockets inside out. Then, he turned back, and bounced up to an imaginary girl — somewhere between goofy and suave.

"Hi!" he said, making his voice much more quick and animated than usual. "Can I have your baby? I mean — do you want *my* baby? I mean — I mean — let's make babies *together,* that's what I mean. I mean — " He stopped, looking slightly confused. "I want a candy bar. I gotta go get a candy bar." He wandered bouncily away.

Jankowski found this a lot funnier than Snoopy did.

"No way," Snoopy said. "The young ladies like to follow me everywhere, is what *I* think. I get even one minute to myself, and I'm lucky as can be."

Michael and Jankowski both laughed.

"Okay, okay," Snoopy said. "Who am I." He sat very still, his legs lounging out in front of him, very solemn, and completely expressionless. And — he stayed that way.

"*Viper*," Michael and Jankowski said, and they all laughed.

"Here's another," Snoopy said, and put on a serious expression, standing up very straight. "Here," he said, calmly, "is what we're going to do, and here is where we're going to do it, and — Snoopy? Is something funny? No, I didn't think so — here is exactly *how* we're going to do it, and here is how long it's going to take."

"Sounds like the Sarge to me," Jankowski said, laughing.

And — it really *did* sound like Sergeant Hanson. Snoopy was pretty damned good at this.

"Correct," Snoopy said, very serious. "Now, then. Let's start by — *Meat*. Wake up, Meat! — let's start by — "

"What's going on?" a voice behind them asked. A very calm and serious voice.

Oh, no. Talk about red-handed. Michael busied himself with what was left of his coffee.

"We were just having lunch, Sarge," Snoopy said, looking very innocent, and Michael and Jankowski nodded. Guiltily.

"Well, why don't you get back to work now,"

Sergeant Hanson said. His voice was pleasant, but it was definitely an order. "That hole isn't going to get dug by itself."

Jankowski got up. "You're right, Sarge," he said.

"Yep," Snoopy said. "We better get to it."

Michael reached for his entrenching tool. "Don't start without me," he said.

And, they all started digging again.

And they dug, and they dug, and they dug. After a while, it started drizzling, but they just kept digging. The rain helped a little, actually. Softened up the ground some.

"Think we'll be sleepin' under the stars tonight," Snoopy said.

"What stars?" Michael asked. His blisters hurt. His back hurt. He felt grouchy as hell. "I never see stars in this stupid country."

"I think our little friend Meat is getting tired," Snoopy said to Jankowski, who nodded.

Michael just grumbled, and kept digging.

"Is it your monthly menstrual time?" Snoopy asked sympathetically.

Michael had to laugh.

"I get the curse *awful* bad," Snoopy said to Jankowski. "Have to stay in bed for near a week."

What a jerk. Michael shook his head. "And you think *I'm* pathetic."

"I lie there, in bed," Snoopy said sadly — he wasn't exactly getting much digging done, at the moment — "and my mother pulls the shades down, and puts a cool washcloth on my forehead."

Hunh. "Your mother does that?" Michael said. "Mine does, too."

Jankowski stared at both of them, his hair wet from the rain and all spiky around his face. "Your mothers do that when you guys get the *curse*?"

Snoopy looked shy. "I feel better just calling it my monthly."

Michael ignored him. "No — when I get a cold," he said to Jankowski. "Or the flu or something." And thinking about it made him, yet again, very homesick. His mother tended towards serious hovering when any of them got sick — and even when she *had* to know that they were faking it a little, she was still right there, fluffing pillows, cooking soup, and going out to the grocery store to buy them what she called "junky magazines." His brother Dennis called them "*lit*-tra-ture." Dennis was, by far, the best faker in the family. Stayed home from school the most.

"If you say so." Jankowski went back to digging.

Michael grinned. "When I get the curse, she brings me chocolate."

"I get powerful, *awful* cramps," Snoopy said, sadly. "Like to die from."

Jankowski just shook his head, and dug. The hole was well over knee-deep now — and very muddy. The mud kept caking to their shovels, making them feel twice as heavy.

Finnegan and Viper came ambling over, apparently having been freed from their other work detail.

"Call this a hole?" Finnegan asked, drinking a can of beer.

"We call it a mud puddle," Snoopy said. "Where'd you get the brew?"

Finnegan gestured back over his head. "Resupply came in. We got hots coming, too." He looked up at the rain. "Maybe." Hots, being hot food, flown out to troops in the field in insulated green containers. Occasionally.

"We allowed to knock off?" Snoopy asked.

Finnegan shrugged. "We make our bed, and we lie in it."

Michael looked down at the mud. He could hardly wait. Beer, on the other hand, might improve his mood. Not doing any more digging today would improve it even more. Snoopy was putting his entrenching tool down, so he put his down, too, ready to follow him.

"More to do here," Viper said, before they could leave.

Well — yeah, but it wasn't like they were going to be able to finish it today — not by any stretch of the imagination. Michael stopped walking, anyway. Viper was big. He didn't mess with Viper.

"Not much light left," Jankowski said.

Viper nodded, unfolding his battered entrenching tool. "Let's get it sloped," he said. "Ground cover. Put some ponchos up."

Nobody argued. They picked up their shovels, and got to work.

CHAPTER 10

RESUPPLY didn't make it in with any hot food — somehow, Michael wasn't surprised — so, he made do with a can of warm beer, and a can of almost warm ham and limas. Finnegan gave him some Tabasco to put in it, which helped. A little.

He and Snoopy were assigned to LP — Listening Post — that night, between 2100 and 2400. Pretty slack, as night duty went. LPs went out beyond the perimeter, sat down — in this case, on a couple of empty wooden crates that had once held artillery rounds — and listened. They carried a radio with them, and if they heard something — anything — they would whisper a report to the CP. LPs weren't bad, because they were usually dull, but if something *did* happen, they were terrible, because whoever was out on the LPs got caught in the crossfire.

The scariest part, actually, was creeping out there in the dark. Down the hill, avoiding the concertina wire and claymores. It was still drizzling, and they sat underneath a piece of canvas Snoopy had scrounged somewhere. In the rain, canvas was a lot better than using plastic, or ponchos, because the rain made less noise landing on it. Made it easier to hear, and less easy to be *heard*. It also made it a lot easier to get drenched — but they already were, so it didn't matter much.

They weren't supposed to talk — for obvious reasons — but it was so lonely and quiet out there, sitting in the jungle, in the rain, that it was hard not to.

"Hate this," Snoopy said.

Michael nodded, so wet that his uniform was plastered against him. His boots felt like they might rot right off his feet.

They sat there. It wasn't raining hard enough to discourage the mosquitoes, but just hard enough to wash off the bug juice as fast as they could rub it on.

"I'm a *good* ski teacher," Michael said. "Especially kids. I like teaching little kids." And — he did. Always had.

Snoopy laughed. Very quietly. "Knew you were mad about that."

Michael nodded.

They sat there. They got wetter.

"I would *never* take a candy bar over a girl," Snoopy said.

Michael nodded. Neither would he. Not even a frozen Milky Way. Unless she was a very, very unpleasant girl. And even then — he would think twice.

They sat there. They watched. They didn't see anything. They didn't hear anything. They keyed the handset of the radio twice every hour on the half hour.

"I hate this," Snoopy said.

Michael nodded.

"I hate this a lot," Snoopy said.

Michael nodded.

They sat there.

Over the next few days, they spent almost every waking hour digging. Except when they were chopping down trees, and dragging logs up the damned hill, to build overhead cover. Half the time, the logs were so heavy — and, often, slippery with rain — that someone would let go, the thing would roll down twenty or thirty or a hundred feet, and they would have to drag it back up again. If they were lucky, they got day-time perimeter guard, which was boring — lately, anyway — but not exactly taxing.

They pulled night ambush one night, LP the

next, bunker guard the night after that. Sometimes it rained; sometimes it didn't. Sometimes
people thought they saw things; sometimes they
didn't. Sometimes people would shoot up flares;
sometimes people would throw grenades — but
nothing ever came of it. Almost no incoming.
Lots of outgoing.

Sometimes, they got hot food. Mostly, they
didn't. Sometimes, a load of supplies would miss
the landing zone, and they would have to drag
it uphill, grunting and swearing a lot. Delta Company was brought in, and started digging
hootches of their own, a good week behind
Alpha and Echo. Bravo and Charlie would be
coming in too, but no one knew when. Everyone
knew that a battalion-sized operation was coming, but no one knew when that was going to
happen, either. Or where.

Michael was in no hurry.

Being at the firebase was pretty boring — not
that he was complaining — and it was harder
than usual to keep track of time. Except Mon-
days. When Doc gave them big orange malaria
pills, instead of their usual small ones, that meant
that it was Monday. That another week had gone
by in Vietnam. He'd only had one at the firebase
so far, so he knew they hadn't been there as long
as it seemed.

They would dig all day — they had started their second hootch, even though the first one wasn't quite finished yet — and then, stop about an hour before dark to write letters, read letters, eat C-rations, smoke cigarettes. A lot of guys took advantage of every break to grab some sleep. No one ever got enough, and everyone was always tired.

It was very late afternoon, and pretty quiet, except for helicopters landing now and again, and the odd fire mission here and there. Nothing unfamiliar, nothing alarming. And — Michael was taking a break.

Their hootch had two layers of sandbags stacked on top of the timbers, and when they got another layer put on there, they would be pretty much done. It was at least five feet deep, with sandbags stacked another four or so feet above the ground. Plenty of headroom. They'd made some bunks out of empty ammo crates, and Jankowski rigged up a little light with a radio battery and a couple of bulbs he'd gotten from a guy he knew at the commo shack. The commo shack was made out of a metal conex box, which was a huge shipping crate. The outside was layered with sandbags, and inside, it was full of radios, monitored twenty-four hours a day. Going in there after walking around the primitive firebase felt like entering a cramped space-ship. All lights, and static, and disembodied voices.

Snoopy was down inside the hootch, "check-ing the acoustics," which really meant that he was taking a nap. Word had it that 1st Platoon was going out on patrol the next day — but no one knew if it would just be a couple klicks and then, back to the firebase, or if they'd be out there for a while. So even though he was pretty damn tired and should probably go down and crash out for a while, Michael decided that this would be a good time to write a letter home. Write a bunch of lies about how there was no need to worry about him or anything. Besides, truth was, being cooped up in a dank, dirt hole in the ground kind of gave him the creeps. Felt like a tomb.

But, his ruck was down there, and he needed some paper and a pen. They had dug little steps in the dirt, and left a gap in the sandbags for a door. There were other, much smaller gaps, to serve as firing positions. Should the need arise.

It was dark down there — smelled like a locker room after a *very* ugly football defeat — and Michael had to wait for his eyes to adjust before he could see. Snoopy was sound asleep, his face in the dirt. Michael would have stuffed a flak jacket under his head, for a pillow, but he didn't want to wake him up, so he just got his paper and pen and went back outside, as quietly as he could.

He sat down in the dirt, leaning his M-16 next to him, up against the side of the hootch. His paper — each platoon got stationery and candy and stuff in the sundries package that came every week or so — was wrinkled, and had a couple of water spots, but, hey — there *was* a war on. He couldn't exactly go down to the drugstore and buy more.

Dear Mom and Dad, he wrote.

Good start. Where to go next, was the question. He hadn't told them much of anything that was true yet — especially not about what happened with J.D., or the guy who got his hand blown off by a mine, or the guy who got bitten by a rat, lost a chunk of his face, and had to be flown to the rear for a series of rabies shots. Hadn't told them anything like that.

No reason to start now.

It's still raining a lot here, but they say it gets worse when the monsoons start. I

*don't really know when that is, but I think
it's soon. It gets pretty hot, and I have a
weird-looking tan.*

He also had the beginnings of some jungle
rot — the worst was the rash starting to spread
under his arms; disgusting; itched like hell —
and his hands had blisters on top of blisters.
Not that he was complaining. Hell, no.

*We've been doing a lot of digging lately,
and made an underground hootch to sleep
in. Reminds me a little of playing fort with
Dennis and Joey.*

Joey had been his best friend, growing up. His
family had moved back East — New England,
or some damn place — and although they'd
pretty much lost touch, he was guessing Joey had
ended up in college somewhere. No way would
he have let himself get drafted. Get into this mess.

*I hope Otis is okay. He does miss me,
right?*

He didn't want his dog to be unhappy — on
the other hand, he would be sort of sad if Otis

was just scampering around, fetching sticks, without a care in the world, not even noticing that his favorite person wasn't around anymore.

I've got good guys in my squad, especially Snoopy. (He's the one who wrote something in that first letter — I hope you got it — but he signed it with his real name, Robert Baker.) No one ever calls him that, though. He's pretty funny. Keeps everyone laughing.

And he hoped like hell that everything would be okay, and they would get to meet him someday. Get to meet all of these guys. That *he* would still see them, sometimes.

I'm fine. We don't get much sleep, so sometimes I'm tired —

Sometimes?

— but otherwise, I'm fine.

He didn't know what else to say. It was his *family*, he should know what to say. But — they knew he wasn't a writer guy. And it wasn't like he could tell them the *truth*. His mother was worried enough, as it was.

So, don't worry about me.

Goat, a guy from Delta Company he'd met the other day when they were next to each other in line at the water trailer, walked by with two other guys.

"How ya doin', Meat?" he said. He was wearing a Yankees cap. *Always* wore it, apparently.

"Just gettin' some rays," Michael said, gesturing towards the sun. He was getting — gettin' — this habit of dropping his *g*'s, when he talked to certain kinds of guys. It was contagious.

The guys continued down the hill. They all had machetes, so they must be on their way to get another log. Fun.

Michael looked down at his letter. It was pretty boring, but he didn't know what to write. It wasn't like he sat around swapping yarns all the time. Little tales he could share with his loved ones.

Say hi to Dennis and Carrie. I'll write you again soon.

Love, Mike

Well — it was the best he could do. He looked at the letter for a minute, then decided to add one more thing.

> *P.S. If you see Elizabeth again, don't give her my address, okay? Thanks.*

Kind of a grim note to end on. But, at least he didn't have to explain to them *why* he didn't want her writing to him. They knew what she was like.

> *Sorry the paper is a mess — our hootch leaks. We're not too good at building, I guess.*

It was a stupid letter. He folded it up, then sealed and addressed the envelope, and stuck it in his pocket. Outgoing mail sacks were kept up near the commo shack and the FDC, and he'd take it up there later.

He looked around. Still pretty quiet. C-4 explosions, as guys blew trees. Lots of metal clinks as shovels hit rocks. Even more swearing. He and Finnegan had LP tonight. Before, Finnegan had been the biggest talker in the squad — more of a motor-mouth than Snoopy, even — but he still wasn't talking much these days. He'd started playing his radio again, though — just didn't sing along anymore. Not even to the Doors. It was sad to watch.

Sitting in the sun was boring. And hot. He could go dig some more, but he didn't feel like it. At all. Viper was sitting on a small crate, next to what was going to be their other hootch, smoking, and cleaning his M-60. So, Michael wandered over. What the hell.

"Got any tape?" he asked. He could spend some time taping his magazines together, maybe.

Viper jerked his thumb in the direction of the hole. "Janny does," he said, the cigarette barely moving as he spoke.

Michael looked in the hole and saw Jankowski curled up in the bottom, sound asleep. His face in — where else — the mud. Jesus. Talk about depressing. He took off his helmet and sat on it, lighting a cigarette of his own.

"You think they know, in the World, there's kids lying in the jungle, using mud for a pillow?" he asked.

"Don't think they care," Viper said.

Even more depressing. But, probably true. They were all cruising around in cars, going to football games, eating buckets of hot buttered popcorn at the movies. Doing whatever they wanted, whenever they wanted. Figuring any guy dumb enough to get himself sent to Vietnam wasn't worth worrying about. What did they care, as long as *they* got out of it?

He smoked his cigarette. The smoke was hot. *He* was hot. They sat there, Viper's full concentration on the barrel of the M-60.

"Got any pictures?" Michael asked.

Viper's concentration wavered only slightly.

"Of your baby," Michael said.

Viper nodded, and kept cleaning the gun.

Oh. Okay. "Good," Michael said. "That's good. That you have pictures."

Viper frowned a little, then unbuttoned a pocket in his fatigue pants, handing him a black and white picture of a tiny, bald, toothless, smiling baby, lying on its stomach, wearing nothing but a diaper.

"Cute," Michael said. "He has your eyes."

"She," Viper said.

Oh. "She has your eyes," Michael said.

Viper grinned, took the picture back, and rebuttoned it into his pocket. They sat there, smoking.

"Nice weather we're having," Michael said.

Viper nodded.

Didn't look like this conversation was going anywhere. "Well," he said, and got up.

"Don't aim to make friends here," Viper said.

"We talked 'bout this, you and me. So — don't take it personal."

Michael nodded.

"I meet you back in the World someday, down the Piggly-Wiggly, then yeah, you and me'll have us some Budweiser," Viper said. "Find out 'bout ourselves. Might be, we'll get along real good. In fact, hope we do. That'd be just fine."

Michael thought about that. "What's the Piggly-Wiggly?" He *knew* what Budweiser was.

Viper frowned. "Where you from, you don't know Piggly-Wiggly?"

Michael frowned back. "That's getting kind of personal, don't you think? I mean, hey, come on now."

"Yeah." Viper picked up an extra M-60 barrel and started cleaning it, too. "Can't think what came over me."

"Well — just don't let it happen again," Michael said.

Viper grinned. "Count on it," he said.

CHAPTER II

It was two days before Thanksgiving. More importantly, it was two days before the first real milestone Michael had had — one month, in-country. The strangest, most intense, most mind-bending month of his life.

So far, anyway.

After all, it might go and get — boring — on him. In the next two days. On account of the holiday, and all, resupply would probably send out warmish turkey roll, brown floury gravy, reconstituted mashed potatoes. Long as it didn't rain. Seemed to rain constantly. Wait 'til monsoons, everyone kept saying. You ain't seen *nothin'* yet.

1st Platoon was going on day patrol, somewhere out beyond the perimeter, and 1st Squad was going to be on point. Meaning, Michael was going to be on point. First time.

Help.

After stand-to, Lieutenant Brady motioned him over, holding a map and a grease pencil in one hand, and what was left of a cigarette in the other.

"You're okay with this?" he said.

No. But, Michael nodded.

"I don't force anyone," Lieutenant Brady said. "That's not how I operate."

Which wasn't going to get him too many promotions. The Army *liked* forcing people to do things. He was aware that Lieutenant Brady was looking at him. Closely. So — he'd better say something.

"No problem, L-T," Michael said. "Can do." Was he a good American, or *what*. Make his Uncle Sam proud, damn it.

Lieutenant Brady looked a little worried — but, then again, he *usually* looked a little worried. And a lot tired. A guy who should be home in Virginia, or wherever, with a nice blonde wife and a white picket fence. "Okay," he said. "Bubba wants to go over a few things with you."

Bubba? "Sir?" Michael said.

"Sergeant Hanson," Lieutenant Brady said.

Oh. Michael grinned. Bubba. How about that. He walked over to Sergeant Hanson, who was making one of the new guys — amazing, now, that there were a bunch of guys here newer than *he* was — jump up and down, then taping or tying down everything that rattled or clinked. All business. The war is not a toy, son.

"Uh, Sergeant Bubba?" he said, and grinned again.

Sergeant Hanson's gaze flickered slightly. "You're all set, kid," he said to the new guy. "Remember, easy on the water, and take your salt pills. You'll be right behind Smitty, and you do what he does. You'll be fine."

The guy nodded with wide eyes — he was pudgy and freckled; probably from a tiny town in Ohio, Michael was guessing — and he moved away, clumsy under the weight of his rucksack.

"Cherries, man," Michael said, and shook his head.

Sergeant Hanson gave him a hard little push. "Shut up, kid."

Right. Michael grinned. *Bubba,* of all things.

Sergeant Hanson pushed him again. "I want your full attention here, Meat."

Right. Michael looked attentive.

"Okay." Sergeant Hanson let out his breath. "Like the L-T said, today's just a simple cloverleaf." Which meant that the route they would walk would be in that general pattern. "You and me, we're going to switch off every hour. You start heading in the wrong direction, I'll haul you back."

Michael nodded. Nothing to dwell on, but his throat was kind of starting to hurt. Kind of a lot.

"Use your gut," Sergeant Hanson said. "It's almost always going to be right. Something feels funny, you stop. We're not trying to set any speed records here."

Michael nodded. His throat hurt. It was going to be hard to swallow. Already was.

"Look for anything that doesn't look right," Sergeant Hanson said. "Doesn't seem natural. They usually leave signals for each other. Some small slashes on a tree, a couple, three twigs on the ground, a little piece of rope tied to a vine."

Michael nodded. He was completely out of his league here.

"Or — " Sergeant Hanson shrugged. "Maybe the ground's chopped up a little. Or a branch is broken off funny. You want to look low, but don't forget to look high. Especially vines. Overhanging branches. Don't take anything for granted. Okay?"

Michael nodded. His throat might, it felt like, just close right up.

"They're good, Meat," Sergeant Hanson said, "but they're not *that* good."

J.D. had been good. Real good. But, Michael nodded.

"Okay. Start off at slack." Sergeant Hanson turned towards the rest of the platoon. "Rucks on, guys. Let's saddle up!"

There was the usual mumbling and grumbling, but then, they were moving out, Sergeant Hanson in the lead. There was one break in the perimeter, where the rolls of concertina wire stopped, forming a little opening. The gate. Guarded, of course, around the clock.

They moved through the gate, and down the hill. It was early, and it was hot. At least *he* was hot. He was perspiring. Heavily.

Sergeant Hanson took them down the hill, then across it. Slowly. This whole hump was going to be in the hills. The jungle. No valley, no paddies, probably no villages. Just jungle. Trees on top of trees on top of trees, the jungle floor dark below. Hot. Always hot. Vines and brush and bamboo and thorns. Everywhere.

Michael tried to watch the jungle *and* Sergeant Hanson. His hands were perspiring so much that his gun felt slippery. And his throat felt — thick. Swollen. Sergeant Hanson would pause, and he didn't know why. Listening? Seeing? Everything looked okay to him.

It didn't seem like they had been walking very long, but they were stopping now. Taking a break. A few gulps of water, maybe a salt pill. Michael didn't want to talk to anyone, so he sat by himself, on his helmet, knocking off ants that started to climb up his boots, brushing away bugs that flew in his face.

The big game. He should pretend he was getting ready for the big game. Clear his mind. Take slow, deep breaths. Bunch the muscles in his upper body and arms, then release them. Over and over. Always helped him get pumped up. Get those muscles twitching. Get that adrenaline working. Get ready for quick physical reaction. And — clear the mind. Empty it. Get rid of the clutter. Get ready to go.

"Meat," Sergeant Hanson said.

Shit.

"Bear left, slow curve, the next couple hundred meters," Sergeant Hanson said, calmly. "Take your time."

Michael nodded, standing up. He brushed the dirt, and remaining ants, off his helmet, and put it on.

"You're on rock and roll," Sergeant Hanson said. "Anything happens, you let 'er rip."

Michael nodded, taking his M-16 off safety —

and putting it on full automatic. His hands were shaking. Great. He shrugged his shoulders a few times, flexed and loosened the muscles.

Sergeant Hanson smiled at him. "Don't worry, kid. I'm right behind you." Then, he signaled for everyone to move out.

Which they did.

Michael took it slow. An understatement. He was very — aware of himself. Aware of everything. Stay cool. Stay calm. Don't think.

Step at a time. Look at the ground, look to the left, look to the right, look up, look back at the ground. Another step. Then, do it all over again, but look in a different order. Up first. Then, down. Then, around.

He was eighteen years old, he had done nothing of value with his life, and he was in a hot stinking jungle in Vietnam, leading a patrol of twenty guys who were relying on him to do everything right. Jesus Christ. How the hell did he get into this? If he was home right now, he — do *not* think. Look. Watch. *Listen*.

Was the ground rough? Disturbed? Or was it just — *ground*? He was dizzy. His head hurt. His heart seemed to be — maybe because he wasn't breathing. *Breathe*. Holding his breath was just — stupid. Cowardly. Stupid. He shouldn't be out here. He was really stupid. He didn't know what he was doing — and he was a coward. Any second, the ground might explode beneath his feet. Blow him into — it *happened*. He'd *seen* it happen. And — now it was his turn.

He was scared. He was *terrified*. He couldn't do this. He was going to get everyone killed. He wasn't brave enough. He wasn't *smart* enough. Hanson had fucked up big, choosing him.

Step. Step. Hesitate. Step. The jungle seemed — alive. Like all this vegetation might reach out and grab him. Like — like in *The Wizard of Oz*, when the apple trees started — don't think. What would he tell Sergeant Hanson if they got hit right now — sorry, Bubba, I was thinking about the Yellow Brick Road. About the Cowardly Lion. About the song he sang when — *don't* think. Concentrate.

He was perspiring so much that his eyes were stinging, but he was afraid to blink. Afraid he might miss something. Afraid — breathe, already. He had to remember to breathe.

Someone might be looking at him. Right now. From a low bunker, from a high tree. Looking at him through rifle sights, getting ready to aim, fire — he cringed, even though nothing happened. Hunched his shoulders up. Lowered his head a little. But — he didn't want Sergeant Hanson to see. To know he was scared.

Step. Step. Bearing sort of left. How long had he been out here? A week? An hour? A minute? It was just jungle. All he could see was jungle. Nothing but — something moved. To his left. Something — he stopped. Froze. Did *not* breathe.

A snake. Curling slowly along a tree limb. About eye level. Fatly, almost luxuriously, coiling. Did it see him? Was it about to — should he shoot it? What if it — something flashed by him, and the snake's head was suddenly lopped off, Michael ducking away from the spray of blood.

He looked at Sergeant Hanson, who gave him a quick little-kid grin, then winked, and wiped the blood from his machete onto his pants before putting it away.

It was awful. It was big and ugly and bloody, and still seemed to be alive. And — he was scared stiff. Scared to move past it. Scared to do anything. But, stretched out long behind him, the whole platoon was — without stopping to think, he yanked out *his* machete, and slashed the snake again, his arm moving in a fierce, convulsive shudder. The snake — finally realizing it was dead? — was uncoiling very slowly from the branch — then landed with an unexpected

writhing thump on the ground, Michael flinching
in spite of himself. Then, he wiped the blood
across his pantsleg, his skin instinctively shri-
veling away from the moisture.

He felt better. He looked, listened, stepped.
An act of completely pointless brutality — and
he felt better. Felt fierce. The blood was sticky
on his leg, thick and warm, just above his knee,
and he felt — sick. Sick and trembly and jum-
bled — and like a tough son-of-a-bitch nobody
better fuck with.

Nobody.

He stepped. Slow down. Look. Step. Breathe.
Then — do it again. And again. Can do. Will do.
No problem.

When they finally stopped, his legs felt weak,
but he took his time sitting down, not wanting
anyone to know. His pants were stiff where the
blood was, and suddenly afraid for some reason
that he might have gotten some in his mouth, he
spit. Several times. He took a mouthful of water
from one of his canteens, then spit again. Then,
he took a bent C-rat pack of Lucky Strikes out
of his helmet liner and lit one. Smoked it, staring
down at the ground.

The ground. He'd had no idea that dirt could

be so — all-encompassing. So complex. Full of secrets. His mouth still felt funny, and he spit a couple more times.

Snoopy came over and sat down, and he glanced at him, then looked away. He wasn't ready to talk to anyone. To come down yet. To be human again.

"So?" Snoopy said, finally.

"It was a skate," Michael said, and spit again. Because — his mouth felt funny. "Nothin' but a skate."

He and Sergeant Hanson switched on and off, the rest of the day. And Michael switched on and off. Every nerve, every instinct, on edge; then, shutting down. Just staying alert. Backing Sergeant Hanson up. Waiting and watching and ready for anything. Any*one*.

Sometime late in the hot afternoon, Sergeant Hanson found two old abandoned bunkers. He stopped, showing Michael with his hands where the line of the jungle broke, where the growth was different. How the jungle wasn't always just jungle.

Two Squad and Three Squad split to each side, forming defensive flanks, and 1st Squad advanced, weapons off safety, to check the bunkers out. They were empty. Long empty. Full of jungle debris. They were both well on the way to caving in, and Sergeant Hanson and Lieutenant Brady finished the job with some C-4.

And — they moved on. No booby traps. No contact. No anything. Except, maybe, for nerves stretched further than they should have to stretch. Michael was on point for the last part of the day, leading them back up the hill, and in through the break in the wire — and even then, he couldn't relax. Couldn't manage anything other than opening his flak, then putting his rifle on safety, and holding it with only one hand, instead of two. Wiping the other one across his already perspiration-drenched shirt.

Once they were inside the firebase, everyone else seemed kind of cheerful and relaxed, like guys coming out of the factory at quitting time. Michael felt like something explosive, just waiting for a detonator. Felt — very strange.

"Hey, check it out," Snoopy said, pointing up near one of the water trailers. "Field kitchen!"

"*Steaks*," someone else said. "I smell steaks."

A lot of guys instantly looked happy, shedding rucksacks and heading up the hill; but a lot of other guys looked grim.

"It's not good?" Michael asked Jankowski, whose face had gone stiff.

Jankowski lowered his ruck and radio to the

dirt, taking his time. "The only time you get steaks, is when they're sending you into some serious shit the next day," he said.

Oh. "Really?" He looked at Viper for confirmation.

Viper's expression didn't change, but he nodded, and headed towards their hootch, the .60 slung over his shoulder.

"*I* haven't heard anything," Thumper said. "Any of you guys heard anything?"

No one had heard anything.

Was he ready to deal with this? No. Michael headed for their hootch to get rid of his rucksack. To regroup.

"You aren't going to eat?" Snoopy asked. "We should eat."

"The line's too long," Michael said. Made sense, since the whole damned battalion was here. Since they were apparently about to go on the long-rumored battalion-sized mission.

Something big. It must be something big.

Something bad.

Snoopy tagged after him. "We should eat, man. 'Case they run out."

Michael nodded, climbing down the dark steps into the hootch, and dumping his rucksack in the corner. Viper was already in there, lying on his poncho liner on one of the bunks, smoking, and reading a wrinkled letter by the light of a small squat candle. Exactly what Michael felt like doing. But — maybe he wanted privacy. Which was damned hard to find around here. So, Michael just nodded at him, lit a cigarette of his own — only had two left, damn it — and turned to head out.

"Didn't do too bad today," Viper said.

Michael paused, halfway up the dirt steps. "Hard work," he said.

Viper nodded, flipping a page to read the other side. "Doesn't get easier."

Great. Michael started up the steps again, then stopped. "You got a real name, Viper?"

Viper nodded, reading.

"Yeah," Michael said. "Thought you might." He went outside, where Snoopy was waiting impatiently.

"You ready?" he asked, his ruck discarded out in the front of the hootch. "Smells good."

Actually, it didn't. But, Michael followed him up to the long, pretty rowdy line of guys waiting to be served. There was soda and beer, too — two Pabsts per guy — and Michael traded one of his to Timpson, a big cheerful guy in Three Squad, for two Cokes. If tomorrow was going to be bad, it might be a good idea to have a Coke stashed in his ruck somewhere. Couldn't hurt.

Took forever to get served, then he and Snoopy carried their plates back to the hootch, to sit outside and eat in what was left of the light. Finnegan was already there, sitting in the dirt with Moretti, from Two Squad.

"Least they didn't give us ice cream," Finnegan said. "We get ice cream, and we *know* we're headed for it."

Moretti nodded, gnawing at his steak. Looked overcooked. Looked tough. Looked lousy.

Snoopy sat down, cheerful as hell. Making him a minority of one. "I'm a happy young man," he said, using his church key to open one of his beers, then pulling out his K-bar to use on the steak. "They smell great, and they're going to *taste* great."

They didn't.

CHAPTER 12

CA. COMBAT ASSAULT. To secure some damned hill out in the Que Son Mountains. Delta Company would be inserted first, to make the initial assault, with Echo Company right behind them. Alpha and Bravo would be to the north and the west of the hill, to serve as blocking forces. Classic hammer-and-anvil, the officers must be saying, smugly, back at Battalion HQ. Oh, and, Joe, how about some more of that champagne and lobster while you're standing there.

Not that Michael particularly liked either of those things. But, still. Easy for a guy, safe and air-conditioned back in the rear, to make battle plans he didn't have to carry out personally. Anyway. Charlie Company, those lucky sons-of-bitches, was going to stay behind at the firebase, to serve as security.

Battalion intelligence, or brigade intelligence — or, anyway, someone who laid claim to being *very, very* smart — had it that a force of NVA regulars, of unknown size — probably a reinforced company — was using this particular hill as a sort of base camp or staging area or something. So, they were to eliminate, and secure, Hill 568 — the hills were named on the basis of how many meters high they were. Nothing picturesque like Porkchop Hill, or Heartbreak Hill, or whatever.

Be really stupid to get yourself killed on a hill with a number for a name.

The firebase got mortared that night, but nothing too serious — it was more of the "Hi! Remember us?!" variety. Michael had been out on LP with Jankowski, but by the time the rounds started coming in, about 0300, he was already inside the hootch. *Well* inside, trying to sleep with his helmet and flak on, hoping like hell that they wouldn't score a direct hit. But, too tired to worry a whole lot about it. Snoopy, as always, kept his helmet over his crotch, saying, "Well, hell, man, I never *use* my head."

One of the howitzers was pretty much destroyed — not a direct hit, but close, and a few guys got hurt — but nothing life threatening. So Michael heard, anyway. And if it wasn't true — he didn't want to know.

It was raining in the morning, and the cloud cover was very thick. Didn't seem to be changing anyone's plans, though. It was an effort to eat, and most of them didn't. Everyone was cleaning and oiling their weapons — borrowing rods and brushes, if they didn't have their own — and then, doing it again. They were all carrying more ammunition than usual, with extra rounds for the M-79 guys, and almost everyone was wearing a belt of ammo for the M-60s. Light antitank weapons were being handed out — LAWs were good for only one bazooka shot, but they weren't very heavy — and most people took one. Michael, included. He also took a couple of tear gas — CS — grenades, and a few extra frags. He'd a hell of a lot rather have too much ammo, than not enough.

Beyond that, they were taking a couple of canteens each, their ponchos and poncho liners, a few C-rat cans — and not much else. They were each carrying at least one pressure bandage, stuck in their helmet bands. But, mainly, they were carrying ammo. Lots of ammo. And — weapons. Plenty of weapons. Looking around, Michael saw a lot of .45 pistols, a few AK-47s, and even a pump gauge shotgun here and there. Knives, bayonets, and there was even a guy flicking a switchblade open and shut. Over and over.

Nobody was talking much. Not even Snoopy. Although he *was* standing around, eating a can of boned chicken. Seemed to be enjoying it, too.

It was November 22. Four years since Kennedy. Not exactly a good omen.

The five remaining 105s were working non-stop, in an artillery prep of the hill area they were going to, and Michael's ears were ringing a little from all the noise. Fighter bombers were going into the area with a prolonged air strike, preparing possible landing zones and, Michael hoped, blasting hell out of the hill. Scaring away anyone who might be there. The final stage, right before the first troops were inserted, would be gunships going in to completely rocket and strafe the LZ. Saturate it with minigun fire.

Then, as troops landed, whether the LZ was hot or cold, they would spread out in a defensive perimeter, then move out to wherever the Battalion CO decided he wanted them to secure an LZ to be used, ideally, for the duration of the operation — for resupply, possible medevacs, and, with luck, troop extraction — and they would also work to establish the Battalion CP, from which the battle would be directed — mainly, by radio. Then, Delta would lead the assault, Echo Company moving in behind them, as they drove any NVA troops over and off the hill, towards the waiting Bravo and Alpha Companies. The 3/21 — 3rd Battalion/21st Infantry — was supposed to be securing some NVA troop infiltration route a few klicks away, and if the 4/31 needed help, they would be available to reinforce. And, hey — there were always the ARVNs — Army of the Republic of Vietnam — not that any of them had much faith in the South Vietnamese soldiers. So, on paper, this battle plan looked good.

On paper.

Now, they just had to wait. It was raining hard enough so that no one knew if the weather was going to slow things up or not. Or even cancel the entire mission. Operation. Operation Patrick Henry, being its official title. Whatever *that* meant. Could be an allusion — or it could just be some general, wanting to name the operation after his son. They usually named firebases and LZs for their wives. Anyway, if they *weren't* lifted out as scheduled, the entire bombing prep was probably wasted, since any entrenched NVA troops then would have plenty of time to recover.

If *he* were running this damned war, he wouldn't run it like this. Wander around the jungle, and up and down hills? Hell with that. He'd start at the Delta and sweep right on up to Hanoi — and leave it at that.

Not that anyone had asked for his opinion.

So, they waited. In the rain. Not talking much, mainly just leaning against their rucks, smoking or cleaning their rifles — again — or just staring into space. The Battalion Commander had flown in, and was meeting with the Company COs and platoon leaders, in a tense group near the CP. Even *they* didn't seem to know what was going on.

The rain was a sporadic drizzle now, and the artillery prep went on. The meeting by the CP broke up, officers scurrying to confer with NCOs and platoon sergeants, and before long, a lot of sergeants were yelling, "Saddle up! Let's do it!"

Yeah, go, team, go.

They lined up by company, by platoon, and by squad within each platoon. The slicks were coming in now, and they could hear the first squadron long before they could see it, rotor blades thumping in the sky. Then, the slicks were landing, and they were all running, in turn, to board them, heavily weighed down by all the extra ammunition they were carrying.

They lifted off, and out above the valley, heading deep into the Que Son Mountains. Inside his chopper, Michael looked at the rest of the squad. Sergeant Hanson was right by the cargo bay, alert as all hell — gee, really? — staring down at the jungled terrain. Viper was smoking, looking straight ahead at nothing, while Jankowski was leaning back, with his eyes shut. Finnegan had his eyes closed too, and one hand on the St. Christopher's medal he wore on his dog tag chain. He always wore a cross, too. Snoopy was just looking around, to see what everyone else was doing.

The door-gunner and the crew chief, each manning an M-60 on opposite sides of the chopper, looked tense, and ready to start firing at any second. Snoopy was shouting something into Finnegan's ear, and Finnegan stared at him, then Snoopy shouted again. Finnegan looked at him funny, then pulled his battered transistor radio out of his rucksack and turned it on, the volume up all the way.

Armed Forces Vietnam Network, Republic of Vietnam. And — the Beatles. Singing "I Saw Her Standing There."

Everyone looked startled, except for Sergeant Hanson, who looked mad. But — it was kind of funny, and after a few seconds, even Sergeant Hanson was grinning. Especially when Snoopy started singing along, pretending his M-16 was a guitar. The door-gunner joined him, and even though they were on a combat assault, heading into God only knew what, everyone who wasn't singing was laughing. Hard not to.

Not that he knew much about people from other lands — particularly the land he happened to be *in* at the moment — but, *damn,* he loved Americans. Americans were really funny. Had a hell of a lot of heart, Americans did.

Apparently, the LZ was hot, because the M-60s started spitting rounds before they even got there. Before they had a chance to see the red smoke filtering up from a smoke grenade. Red meant hot, green meant cold. This was very definitely red. Time to lock and load.

Finnegan stowed the transistor away, but the song that had been playing after the Beatles and the Rascals was still in Michael's head. Probably in all of their heads. The chopper didn't even come close to landing, hovering six or eight feet above the ground, while they all jumped out. Michael landed hard, badly twisting his knee, and he rolled to his stomach, crawling towards what had to be the perimeter. Other choppers were coming in, there were bullets flying everywhere, his knee was killing him — and yet, as he low-crawled, as fast as he could, through wind-whipped elephant grass, damned if he didn't find himself singing "Georgy Girl." And it wasn't even a song he *liked*. At all.

He could hear AK-47 rounds snapping over his head, but he wasn't sure where they were coming from, so he just kept his head down, and fired back. Gunships flew in, firing up the tree line, and then, he heard someone yelling for them to "Move out!" He looked up enough to see everyone else running forward, crouched low, still firing. So, he pushed himself up, and stumbled forward, so confused that he wasn't even really sure if he was scared. His knee was in bad shape, but there wasn't a whole lot he could do about it at the moment, so he just kept running.

Hey, there, Georgy Girl.

They were being mortared now, and instinctively, he threw himself down to the ground.

"Move out!" someone was yelling. Had to be Hanson. "Move out *now!*"

At first, Michael was too afraid to get up, then he realized that the mortars must be zeroed in on them, and that if they didn't run, they were going to get blown to pieces. So, he staggered up, his knee *really* hurting, and ran like hell for the trees.

The world would see, a new Georgy Girl.

All hell was breaking loose — and he couldn't get the fucking song out of his head.

What was next, "I Enjoy Being a Girl"? No. Petula Clark. He was going to get his head blown off, while singing Petula Clark's Greatest Hits.

"Guns up!" someone was yelling.

"Medic!" someone else was yelling, sounding frantic. "Medic!"

Where was he supposed to go? What was he supposed to do? Everyone was running, and shooting, and they were in the trees now — and he had no idea what was going on.

"Cut it out!" someone yelled. "Hold your fire!"

There was so much shooting, Michael couldn't tell if it was M-16s *and* AK-47s, or just M-16s now.

"Damn it, cease fire!" another voice yelled. "Cease fire!"

Gradually, the firing died down, with the occasional little burst. Everyone around him was breathing hard. Everyone around him was scared. And — it wasn't his squad. It wasn't even his *platoon*. What the fuck was going on?

"Move out!" a voice yelled. "This way!"

"No, this way!" someone else yelled.

There was another burst of fire.

"*Cease* fire!" someone yelled.

They were scrambling up a sort of ridge, falling over rocks and vines and undergrowth. Someone grabbed his arm, and Michael panicked, trying to knock him away — then, realized it was a guy from 2nd Platoon. McSomething.

"Help me!" the guy was yelling. "You gotta help me, man!"

Michael looked down, and saw that he was dragging another guy — a scared, brown-haired kid, who was bleeding from about nine different places.

"I got this arm!" Michael yelled, and they dragged the kid with them, up the ridge. He wasn't very big, but he seemed damned heavy. He also kept yelping with pain, and Michael knew they should be doing something, trying to stop the bleeding — but, he didn't know what, or how, or — he just kept dragging, doing most of the work with his good leg. The kid was thrashing around and moaning a lot, which made it even harder.

"Corpsman!" Michael yelled. "We need a corpsman!"

He could see where they were going now — where the ridge sort of leveled off. There were a lot of guys already up there, chopping out an LZ: on tight guard around the perimeter; and digging in — quickly. Not all of the guys who were digging had entrenching tools, and so, they were using their helmets and K-bars to pry up the dirt.

It was chaos — but it was slightly more controlled chaos. Slightly. Artillery was crashing into the ground, far above them, but the jungle canopy was so thick, he couldn't even *see* the damned hill they were supposed to be taking.

The kid they were dragging seemed even heavier, and Michael realized that he wasn't moving anymore. His neck had flopped over in a weird way, and he and the other guy both realized at about the same time that they weren't dragging a WIA anymore. They stared at each other, not sure what to do, but they had to keep moving, so they dragged him the rest of the way up, tears streaming down the other guy's face. Michael hadn't even known the kid, but he felt like crying, too.

Doc, running around checking everyone, saw them coming and hustled over.

"Put him down!" he said, and as they lowered him gently to the ground, he started to slap pressure bandages on him, then stopped almost as fast, his shoulders sagging.

The guy from 2nd Platoon shoved him. "*Do* something, man. You gotta do something!"

Doc shook his head, patted the guy on the shoulder, then took charge of the casualty himself, dragging him across the clearing to where a couple of other bodies lay, partially covered with ponchos. Then, as someone screamed "Doc!", he hustled off in the direction of the voice.

Michael couldn't not go over there and look at the other bodies, and was relieved that he didn't know either of them. Relieved, and sick. The other guy was just standing there, crying.

"I'm sorry," Michael said.

"Hey! McCormick! Over here!" someone was yelling towards them, and Michael recognized the lieutenant from 2nd Platoon — not that he knew his name.

He steered the guy in that direction. "Do what he says," he said, "okay? Go on over there. I'll cover him up."

The guy nodded, and went stumbling off.

He felt like a ghoul doing it, but he moved the kid's body enough to reach into his bullet-hole-ridden rucksack, and pull out his poncho. He covered him gently with it, then straightened up. Poor guy. Whoever he was.

Then, he stood there, not quite sure what to do next, but a sergeant put an entrenching tool in his hands, pointed, and Michael nodded,

heading towards the group of guys digging a
bunker in the center of the perimeter — presumably for the CP.

"Hey, you! Kid! You hit?"

What? Michael turned, and saw a medic he
didn't know.

"You all right?" the medic asked.

Michael looked down at his knee, and realized
that he must be limping even more badly than
he'd thought. And, that there was a lot of blood
on his uniform. It wasn't his.

"You okay?" the medic asked.

Except for the fact he had just had a kid die
on him while he was trying to pull him to safety.
"Fuck, yes," he said, and kept on walking.

Thumper was one of the guys digging in the
CP, everyone working about ten times faster
than usual. He could hear artillery rounds still
impacting somewhere above them, a lot of people yelling orders, and what sounded like chain
saws, screeching and buzzing over in the direction of the new landing zone.

"Hey," he said to Thumper, having to yell to
be heard, "you seen my squad?"

Thumper looked up, his expression as scared
and confused as everyone else's seemed to be. "I
don't know," he said. "They might be digging
in."

Might.

"Come on!" an NCO behind them ordered. "Let's hustle it up! Get it done!"

Right. Michael let his rucksack fall to the ground, then started digging.

It made as much sense as any of the rest of this.

CHAPTER 13

By 1230, the LZ and CP were considered se-
cured, and Delta Company started off through
the jungle, to make the initial assault on the hill.
Most of Echo Company stayed around the perimeter, setting out claymores, and digging fighting holes — just in case — while a few squads
went out on short patrols, checking for nearby
enemy presence.

1st Squad had just come in from a short, un-
eventful patrol, and Michael was relieved to find
them finally. They all looked hot and tired.

"Hey, there, Georgy Girl," Snoopy said, when
he saw him.

Michael nodded. "Yeah. I've been singing it
too."

"The hell you been?" Sergeant Hanson asked,
frowning at him.

Michael shrugged. He wasn't about to stand
here whining about hurting his knee, and not

being able to keep up. "Ended up with the wrong platoon."

"Okay. From now on, stick close." Sergeant Hanson turned to the others. "Dig in deep. If they don't secure the hill today, we'll be here tonight. One guy digging, one guy on guard. Switch off." Then, he headed for the CP to report in.

Snoopy put his hand out for the entrenching tool, and Michael gave it to him, climbing out of the hole with some difficulty.

"What happened?" Snoopy asked.

"Sprained it." Michael picked up his rifle, and moved out to go on watch. "No big deal."

They hadn't been at it long, when the sounds of clattering automatic weapons and small arms fire broke out somewhere up the trail where Delta Company had gone. All digging stopped, as everyone instantly grabbed for their weapons and dropped to the ground, ready to return fire.

There was a lot of frantic activity around the CP, and then the calls came for 1st, 2nd, and 3rd Platoons to saddle up. Weapons Platoon would remain behind, to secure the perimeter, and give possible mortar support with the 81mm mortar guns they'd humped along. They had also brought a 90mm recoilless rifle, and about twenty-five flechette rounds for it. 3rd Platoon would be carrying it, since word had it that Delta had run into well-fortified NVA bunkers. With the recoilless rifle, they would have a good chance of being able to knock the bunkers out.

The order was for them to leave behind their rucks, and only carry their weapons, ammo, and a couple of canteens. With less weight, they would be able to move more quickly. Instead of going up the same trail, they were going to be fanning out to one side, and coming in to hit the NVA from another direction. Provide enough covering fire so that Delta Company could either push on — or fall back — whichever seemed advisable. Apparently, Delta's point platoon was completely pinned down, and had taken a lot of casualties.

They moved out, 3rd Platoon on point, Michael's platoon bringing up the rear. A few hundred meters out, they ran into a stand of bamboo — nothing but bamboo to be seen in any direction. It could be twenty feet square — it could be as big as a football field — the only way to find out was to plow through it. Or, go around it — but they didn't have time for that. The going was impossibly slow, and the automatic weapons fire off in the distance continued nonstop. Almost none of them had machetes, so they used their knives, each soldier slashing and squeezing through in turn. There wasn't much visibility — beyond the guy just ahead — and vines tangled through the bamboo, everyone's rifle getting caught in them, more often than not.

It took forever and, with noise discipline pretty much destroyed, the company CP ordered anyone with claymores to pass them up. There weren't many, but the point squad set three up, one at a time, blowing the area ahead of them. It speeded their progress — a little.

When they finally broke out of the bamboo, everyone perspiring and out of breath, and started moving through less dense jungle thickets, the front of the column started taking sniper fire. Everyone dove for whatever cover they could find, and fired back — except the fire seemed to be coming from almost every direction. Michael sprayed ground fire in every direction where he was sure Echo Company *wasn't*.

"No, the trees!" Lieutenant Brady yelled. "Look for flashes, then hit the trees!"

Oh. Right. Fire discipline. Michael looked up, trying to forget that he was in a complete panic, then blew off a full magazine at the first muzzle flash he saw. Branches and leaves were shredding off and falling around them everywhere. Like the whole world around them was coming to pieces.

"Everyone up!" Sergeant Hanson yelled. "Keep moving!"

Michael got up, watching the trees, looking for snipers, aware only of what was going on with 1st Platoon. They were advancing through the jungle, and the rest of the company must be, too. Then, suddenly, an incredible barrage of fire broke out up ahead of them. AK-47s, grenades, RPGs — everything. Lieutenant Brady led 1st Platoon out to the left, to bring them up in a flanking maneuver — and then, they started taking fire too. More than Michael had ever seen. Or heard. Like they were up against a whole *regiment* or something. Like they were all going to be killed.

Everyone was crawling forward, returning fire, using trees and fallen logs for cover. Bunker complex. Had to be. Dirt and shrapnel were kicking up all over the place, and Michael rolled up behind a log, taking cover. All around him, people were screaming — orders, or in fear — and there was more than one yell for a medic. Michael pressed hard into the log, making himself as small as he could be, so scared that he was afraid to move.

"Fall back!" Sergeant Hanson was yelling. "Everyone, fall back!"

It was an all-out retreat, everyone crashing

into everyone, and everything, else, and at least two guys stepped on Michael before he got enough nerve to start crawling away himself. There was still so much machine-gun fire that he was afraid to lift his head at all. An RPG thudded into a tree somewhere above his head, and splintered wood and leaves, and shrapnel, landed all over the place, Michael rolling into a ball to try and protect himself.

Was he okay? He was okay. Jesus! He started crawling again, then heard a voice screaming for help somewhere behind him. He stopped, looking around wildly, trying not to lift his head more than a couple of inches off the ground.

"Sarge!" he shouted at the top of his lungs. "Sarge, someone's still out there!" Oh, Christ, was he going to have to go back for the guy alone? Oh, Christ, no. He *couldn't*. He wasn't brave enough. He wasn't brave at all. "Sarge!"

Sergeant Hanson came back in a swift high-crawl.

"We left someone!" Michael said, lying behind what was left of the tree the RPG hit.

There was more screaming for help — it might even be two guys. But, definitely, there was someone out there.

"Oh, fuck." Sergeant Hanson turned. "L-T! Hold the fire mission! 1st Squad, let's go!"

Was he *volunteering* them? No way. No *way* was Michael going out there. It was suicide.

Lieutenant Brady came running over, AK-47 rounds snapping around him, and dove down next to them, his RTO, Manny, right behind him. "What's going on?" he asked, out of breath.

"We got a couple guys out there still," Sergeant Hanson said. "I'll take my squad up and get them."

Wasn't he even going to *ask*? Who the hell did he think he was?

Lieutenant Brady instantly got on the phone, Manny adjusting the frequency as it came in and out. "Echo Six, this is Echo One-Six. Over."

A voice came crackling back. "Echo Six. Go ahead. Over."

While Lieutenant Brady was giving the situation, the rest of 1st Squad had already come hustling over, crawling fast and low.

"Thumper!" Sergeant Hanson yelled. "Move up! And I need a rifleman!"

Thumper and one of the new guys in Two Squad came crawling up. From where he was lying, Michael could see the two casualties now. They were both beyond the fallen logs, just below a little rise. One of them was waving his arm weakly. He couldn't see who they were.

"I'll bring the perimeter up," Lieutenant Brady

was saying. "Three-Six is going to have a squad working the recoilless."

Sergeant Hanson nodded. "Viper, I want the pig there!" He pointed to a spot where two of the logs came together. "Let's move out!"

They all started crawling after him, the rest of the platoon laying down covering fire, rounds crackling everywhere.

"Snoopy, feed him!" Sergeant Hanson ordered, as Viper threw the M-60 into place. "Thumper, you're going to lay 'em out there, fast as you can. Finnegan, Wishbone, give them everything you've got. Keep their heads down!" He ripped a smoke grenade off his web gear. "Who's got green smoke?"

Snoopy yanked one free, and tossed it over.

"Okay." Sergeant Hanson poked his head up over the logs, ducking the immediate hail of gunfire. "Okay," he said, scarily calm. He handed the second green smoke grenade to Michael. "They're out there about twenty-five feet. Leave your rifle here. Try to throw this just beyond them, then follow me!"

What?! Michael stared at him. He had to go *out* there? Lay down fire, okay, but — go *out* there? And not even bring a gun?

Sergeant Hanson threw his smoke grenade, then looked at him. "You coming?"

No! Michael threw his grenade too, green smoke billowing eerily up among all the gun-smoke.

"Don't think!" Sergeant Hanson yelled, and leaped over the logs.

Stupid fucking hero. Michael rolled over the log and after him, in a goddamn *blizzard* of red and green tracers. He moved as fast as he could, hearing — even over all the other noises — his own gulping fear sounds. Sergeant Hanson was already going for the other guy, so Michael grabbed the one who was closer, hooking his arm around the guy's shoulder and neck to try and pull him back.

Oh, Christ. It was Bear. He *knew* Bear.

"I got you, Bear!" he yelled. "Don't worry, I got you!"

The hell he did. Bear was *big*. A lot bigger than he was. He twisted around so that he was on his back, humiliated to hear himself whim-pering a little as bullets kicked up all around him. He got Bear in a sort of hammerlock, and pulled him towards the logs, pushing as hard as he could with his legs to try and propel them forward.

"Switch!" Sergeant Hanson yelled, next to him.

Michael was so scared that he couldn't figure

out what that meant, and Sergeant Hanson yanked him over, moving to take Bear himself. He had been dragging Moretti. *Another* guy Michael knew. Jesus. But — Moretti was much smaller than Bear. Easier to drag.

"*Move!*" Sergeant Hanson yelled.

"Fuck you, Hanson!" Michael yelled back, but he moved, dragging Moretti towards the logs, and suddenly, hands were pulling them over to — relative — safety. Michael was slammed so hard into the dirt that he got the wind knocked out of him, and he lay there, trying to gasp, trying *not* to cry, shaking all over.

"Pull back!" Sergeant Hanson said. "Viper, take the rear!"

Michael was so weak and shaky he wasn't sure he was going to be able to get up, but Finnegan and Wishbone were already dragging Moretti away, and the squad was pulling back.

"Covering fire, Meat!" Sergeant Hanson said, dragging Bear.

Michael fumbled for his rifle, and immediately starting firing in the direction of the bunkers.

"Up!" Viper yelled.

Michael snapped in another magazine, and sprayed the treetops, and they pulled back to the rest of the platoon, and then withdrew in force.

"Perimeter!" Lieutenant Brady said, then

called in a white phosphorus round. He adjusted the fire, then gave the "Fire for effect!" call over the radio. "Let's go!" he yelled to the rest of the platoon. "Pull it back!"

The mortars and artillery gave them enough time to put some distance between them and the bunker complex, since presumably, an air strike would be coming in next. They splashed through a stream, up across the bank on the other side, and up to a small well-protected ridge of land before Lieutenant Brady called for them to halt and form a full defensive perimeter. Everyone responded without hesitation, and Michael could see Doc on the ground in the center, working frantically on Bear and Moretti, behind the cover of some boulders.

The ground was shaking, *he* was shaking, and he was completely ashamed to realize that he was crying. Lying on the ground, pointing his rifle, almost choking on the smells of cordite and rotting vegetation, shaking and crying.

The fuck was wrong with him, he was crying? And — what if someone saw? Found out what a coward he was? He grabbed a handful of dirt, and rubbed it across his face, trying to cover up the tears. Maybe they'd just think he was perspiring. That he was — hot. Yeah, right.

F-4 Phantoms came thundering in, dropping

bomb payloads on the first two passes, trees and rocks and dirt exploding up into the air, whole sections of jungle just ripping apart. The jets dropped napalm on the third pass, the heat from the flames searing up through the jungle towards the ridge they were on. Michael covered his head with his arms, feeling the heat rush over him like a wave straight from Hell.

Right before the gunships came in, Two Squad went hustling away, dragging Bear and Moretti on clumsily assembled stretchers made from ponchos and long sticks. They were going to link up with 3rd Platoon — which had taken a number of casualties — and take the wounded back to the Battalion CP to be evacuated. The rest of 1st Platoon and 2nd Platoon were going to assault the bunkers again.

The gunships fired up the whole area, and then, Michael's platoon and 2nd Platoon moved in. There was more debris around than actual jungle, so while it was hard to keep from falling, it was a lot easier to go forward. And — God knows there were plenty of places to take cover.

They got further this time, firing their weapons every step of the way, and Michael was so sure that all of the air support had wiped the bunkers out, that he was stunned when suddenly, the NVA opened up again from inside their bunkers, firing at them like nothing had ever happened.

They all went down, but kept moving forward, crawling past trees and parts of trees, in and out of bomb and shell craters. The NVA soldiers were throwing Chi-Com — Chinese-Communist — grenades, some of which went off, with small flashing explosions. You couldn't count on it, but Chi-Coms were duds, often as not. Made you feel like buying American, instead of Red Chinese. Feeling slightly protected, crouched down below the dirt lip of a bomb crater, Michael armed and threw back a few grenades of his own. Unless one of their grenades landed in the crater *with* him. But — he wasn't going to think about that.

"LAWs!" Lieutenant Brady shouted. "Take them out!"

Michael had his hanging over his back, and he swung it around, hands shaking as he tried to remember how to fire the damned thing. Finally, he got it loaded and up against his shoulder, then popped up enough to take aim at one of the bunkers, and fire. The weapon had a hell of a lot more kick than he expected, and the force of firing the rocket knocked him down, like a great metal fist had slammed into his shoulder. He crawled back up to the top of the crater, wondering if it had had any effect.

He couldn't tell, but they were shooting, and advancing, so he did too. It was getting hard to see — both from all the smoke, and from the approaching dusk. They had taken out most of the bunkers and spider holes, and were making some headway, when three more bunkers, further up the hill, sent out a hail of bullets and grenades. A lot of guys went down, and he was shocked to see Timpson in Three Squad, who was running up ahead of him, take an RPG in the upper chest, his head and neck instantly disintegrating. So shocked, he fell down right where he was, almost as if it had hit him, too.

Jesus Christ. This was unbelievable.

There was just too much fire to advance, and they were pulling back again, dragging the guys who had gone down, with nothing to show for their two assaults except for a lot of casualties. One of Timpson's arms came off when Michael tried to drag what was left of him, and he fought off a scream, then just dragged him by the other arm, not wanting to be left out there alone. *Anything*, even dragging what had once been a human being with a hell of a sense of humor, was better than that.

So far, Operation Patrick Henry was going just great.

CHAPTER 14

EVERYONE who was still okay — at any rate, still able to walk and function — dragged or carried the most seriously wounded guys, and the KIAs. Michael was dragging what was left of Timpson, wrapped up in his poncho. The guys with less serious wounds made it back down the hill under their own steam. There were so many wounded that only the priority cases were being flown out. The other WIAs were being patched up as much as possible, and the KIAs were just off to one side. Unhappily enough, there was no hurry in their case. Echo Company was now down to less than seventy men — most of whom weren't exactly in top fighting condition.

When Delta Company straggled in, they were in even worse shape. They had had to leave at least ten KIAs behind, and had at least twenty WIAs. Half of the rest of the company looked shell-shocked, and officers were having to give orders two and three times just to get a response.

Dust-offs were having trouble getting in, so a lot of the wounded went out on the resupply choppers, which were dropping slings of C-rations, water, medical supplies — and *lots* of ammo. Including more LAWs and 90mm recoilless rifles, with plenty of rounds. A clear sign they were going to be going right back up that hill in the morning. Although people were hungry and thirsty, they went for the ammo first, taking *more* than they could carry. Michael was no exception to this.

His knee was so swollen and weak that he was having trouble walking, but — hell with it. He was doing better than most of these other guys. He reached back for one of his canteens, to take a drink, and found it empty. Empty, because there was a bullet hole in it. He just threw it away, and drank from his other one instead. Hell with it.

His squad was still in relatively good shape. Jankowski had taken some shrapnel in one arm, which was bandaged up, and Viper's right hand was thickly bandaged, too, after having gotten burned while changing the melted barrel on his M-60. Neither of them was complaining. Finnegan seemed to be all right, except for some bad branch scratches across one side of his face, and Snoopy just looked tired. Sergeant Hanson seemed to be hunching over slightly, but he didn't volunteer any information — and Michael didn't ask. Truth was, he was still pretty pissed off at him for almost getting him killed. For not giving him any choice.

It would be dark soon, and there was so much cloud cover that there wouldn't be any night visibility at all. Great.

"Dig in, deep as you can," Sergeant Hanson said, sounding as though he were losing his voice. "We're going to get hit, and we're going to get hit hard. Stand-to, right before first light."

"We going up again?" Snoopy asked.

"What do *you* think?" Sergeant Hanson asked, and walked away.

Nobody said anything. Wasn't a whole lot *to* say. Then, Viper just shook his head, went over to his hole, and started digging. Nobody else moved.

"I'll go get us some C-rats." Michael bent and picked up an empty sandbag. "And a bunch more grenades."

His knee buckled after a few steps, and he was so tired that he had a hard time getting up. Someone put a hand out to help him, but when he saw that it was Sergeant Hanson, he pushed it aside.

"Don't do me any favors," he said.

"Fine." Sergeant Hanson stepped back, and waited for him to get up. "You have Doc check that out?" he asked, when Michael was standing again, most of his weight on his right leg.

"The fuck's it matter to you?" Michael asked.

Sergeant Hanson shrugged, and the way he was standing made it obvious that he was in some pain, too.

"You hurt, or what?" Michael asked. Not without hostility.

Sergeant Hanson looked at him, completely expressionless. "Go wherever you were going, then get the hell back to your hole," he said, then turned to walk away.

"If you'd *asked* me," Michael said after him, "I would have come with you. But when it's a fucking suicide mission, you're supposed to *ask*."

Sergeant Hanson stopped. "No," he said. "I'm supposed to make a split-second decision, and *you're* supposed to do what I tell you."

Oh, so he was being accused of being a coward now? Michael scowled back at him. "I *did* do what you told me."

"Then I guess I made the right decision," Sergeant Hanson said.

Oh. Hmmm. Michael looked down, wishing that his knee hurt less so he could kick at the ground. "You *still* should've asked," he said, as grumpily as possible.

"Yeah," Sergeant Hanson said. "They *always* ask on *Combat*."

As a matter of fact, they always did. Michael gave the ground a kick. It hurt like hell. But, he wasn't about to groan or anything — no way — so, instead, he spit. It was, after all, what he did best.

Sergeant Hanson grinned, and reached up for the pack of cigarettes in his helmet band. Except — it was almost completely shredded. Obviously, a bullet had come damned close to his head. He frowned, checked his front pockets, then looked over. "Got a cigarette, kid?"

Kid. "Sure, Bubba," Michael said, and took down his own pack, pulling out two very bent cigarettes. They should probably be practicing light discipline now, but they lit up, anyway. Hell with it. Besides, there were enough artillery illumination rounds going up to make the whole area seem strangely back-lit. Creepy. Unreal-looking.

"They going to be okay?" Michael asked.

Sergeant Hanson nodded. "Doc says Bear, for sure, and Moretti, if they got him out quick enough."

Good. Very good. Michael nodded, too.

They smoked.

"What about you?" Michael asked.

Sergeant Hanson shrugged, but he was still hunching. "Took a round in one of my ammo packs," he said. "Cracked some ribs, maybe."

Michael nodded, and they smoked some more.

"You and Snoopy be careful tonight," Sergeant Hanson said. "I think we're in for a bad one."

Right. Michael nodded, and walked — limped — towards the ammo dump. His knee hurt. His knee hurt a lot.

There was another guy standing over one of the crates, taking as many grenades as he could handle, too. He had extremely pale blond hair, and looked very young. There wasn't a bartender in the world, would serve him a beer.

"You Delta Company?" Michael asked.

The kid gave him a dazed sort of nod.

"You know Goat?" The one guy in Delta Company he really knew. Goat, and that damned Yankees cap.

The kid looked at him with odd, old eyes, then nodded.

Unnerving, those eyes. "You seen him?"

"Fuckin' bought it, first five minutes," the kid said. "He was on point."

Oh. Michael felt more tired than he could ever

remember being. So, he just nodded, and bent down for some frags.

On his way back to their position, with an armload of C-rat boxes, and a bag of grenades, he ran into Doc. Safe bet, that Sergeant Hanson had sent him over. Doc, whose uniform — even in the dim illumination — was clearly drenched with blood, frowned at him.

"You as fucked up as you look?" he asked.

Michael shook his head.

Doc frowned some more. "You lying to me?"

Michael shook his head.

Doc looked him over, then nodded. "Good."

"Is Hanson okay?" Michael asked. "I think he's hurt."

"He says he's fine," Doc said. "You're all real stubborn bastards." He turned to go back to the area set aside for the wounded. The ones who hadn't been lifted out yet were probably stuck until first light — and Doc wasn't going to be getting much sleep tonight. Not that any of them were.

"You eat?" Michael asked.

Doc shook his head. "No time, kid."

Kid. "Eat," Michael said, pushed a C-ration box into his hands — one of the good ones; boned chicken — and continued on his way over to his squad.

Lieutenant Brady was there, inspecting their positions, checking fields of fire, making sure they had set out their claymores and trip flares. Making sure that their holes were *extra* deep.

"I want at least three of the five of you alert at all times," he said, "and full-alert from 0200 on. Try not to give away your positions, or shoot off any flares. You hear something, you go with grenades. LPs won't be in until first light."

They all nodded.

Lieutenant Brady nodded, too. "Keep your heads down," he said, and moved on to the next two positions.

It was quiet. Viper and Snoopy went back to digging; Finnegan and Jankowski went back on alert. He and Snoopy were sharing one hole, and the other three would be in the other one. Michael divided up the C-rats and grenades, then took the entrenching tool from Snoopy, digging a grenade sump, and a sort of hollow they might be able to press into if the shelling got really bad. Then, since digging wasn't all that great for noise discipline, he put the entrenching tool down.

"You eat first," Snoopy whispered, on guard.

Michael nodded, quietly ripping open one of the boxes. It was too dark to see what it was — and they all smelled pretty much alike to him — so, he didn't know what it was until he took the first bite. Beef and potatoes. He wasn't hungry, but he forced it down, hoping that it wasn't going to come right back up again. The potatoes always tasted kind of uncooked, and they were worse cold. He finished, then tapped Snoopy's leg, standing up to take over.

"I'm not hungry," Snoopy whispered.

The best indication of all, maybe, that they were in a real bad situation here. "Neither was I," Michael whispered back.

Snoopy hesitated, then sat down in the bottom of the hole to eat. Michael felt for the row of frags, made sure the pins were all straightened for easy access, then felt for the clackers that detonated their claymores. He checked to make sure he had two taped back-to-back magazines in his M-16, then set a few more out in front of him.

If they attacked *this* part of the perimeter, they were in for one hell of a fight.

It was cold. Seemed that way, anyway. Artillery went off all night long, and what sounded like air strikes, too. Right before midnight, mortars started landing outside the perimeter, and the weapons guys started firing their 81mm mortars back.

The noise was unreal, and Michael and

Snoopy huddled in the bottom of their foxhole, trying to squeeze into the little hollow Michael had dug earlier. Only, now there were explosions coming into the compound that sounded different. Whooshing, sort of.

"RPGs!" Snoopy yelled. "They're coming in!"

They both jumped up, just in time to see satchel charges land, maybe fifty meters out in the jungle. Sappers. They were coming in with some goddamn sappers. Trying to overrun the perimeter.

"Grenades only!" Lieutenant Brady shouted, rushing past their position. "Wait on the claymores!"

The whole perimeter was alive with explosions, and in the weird, flickering light, Michael could see shadows out in the jungle. Every time he saw one, he threw a grenade at it — and was damned glad he had plenty of extras.

Somewhere down the line, a guy panicked and fired his machine gun, RPGs zeroing in on the position right away, and there were screams in the bright orange flash.

"Meat," Snoopy said — and it was all so crazy that Michael couldn't tell if he was shouting, or whispering. "We're not going to get out of this, Meat."

"Yeah, well, they aren't, either," Michael said, and kept throwing grenades.

The grenade battle continued at fever pitch for what was either hours, or seconds, and then, the NVA suddenly pulled back, which meant that they must have taken a hell of a lot of casualties. Good.

Except for American mortars, it was quiet for a while, then the NVA mortar attack heated up again, more rounds impacting inside the perimeter this time. There were a couple of direct hits in the mortar guns section, and Michael heard screams of pain, and shouts for medics. And — there was nothing he could do about it. Except listen.

After a while, he heard gunships, and they must have knocked the NVA guns out, because the barrage stopped. More gunships came and fired on the jungle around the perimeter, miniguns spitting out streams of red tracers.

Nobody had to come and tell them to stay on full-alert, but around 0415, Sergeant Hanson came crawling over.

"0500, light up the whole perimeter," he whispered. "We're going to give anyone who's out there a little surprise."

They nodded, only able to see each other in

the brief light of artillery flares, well up above them on the hill.

"Anyone hurt bad?" Snoopy whispered.

"Two KIAs," Sergeant Hanson whispered back. "The others'll make it 'til first light. Look alive, okay?" He crawled on to the next hole.

Michael and Snoopy watched the jungle, both trembling, waiting for whatever was going to come next.

"I miss my dog," Michael whispered.

Snoopy laughed quietly, gave his arm a little pat, and looked out at the perimeter.

"I miss my dog a lot," Michael said.

At 0500, they lit up the jungle with a burst of grenades and machine-gun fire — one long mad minute — and, as usual, had no idea whether it had any effect. Maybe they'd knocked out a bunch of guys; maybe there was no one there. And, they would never know, either way.

By 0530, they were assembled in the defensive stand-to around Lieutenant Brady, to get their morning briefing.

"Arty's going to prep until 0650, and then, the Phantoms are going to Snake and Nape — " drop five-hundred- and one-thousand-pound bombs, in addition to napalm — "until 0800,"

Lieutenant Brady said, "which is when we move out. 2nd Platoon's taking the point, and Delta's going to move out right after us. Bravo had a lot of contact on the north side last night, so they were either reinforcing or bugging out. They're going to hold in position, and we've got some ARVNs coming in to block with them. At first light, Alpha's going to start coming around the mountain, and try to link up with us by 1200."

It was quiet for a few seconds.

"Will they be riding six white horses?" Snoopy asked.

Everyone was too tense to laugh — but, there were a lot of smiles, and Michael tried to picture Alpha Company coming 'round the mountain, riding six white horses. Although the Army would probably dye the horses OD. And give them ill-fitting saddles.

"I hope so, Snoopy," Lieutenant Brady said. "Washington, Fish, you two take the recoilless for now, and I want everyone else carrying at least one round. No rucks, but all the ammo you can hump. Charlie and Delta from the 3/21 are going to be inserted at a new LZ about seven hundred meters east of here, and they'll be joining the assault." He paused. "Any questions?"

Plenty. But Michael didn't ask any, and neither did anyone else.

"Okay," Lieutenant Brady said. "Be ready to move out, then. Your squad leaders'll brief you on anything else." He paused. "We're going to take this hill, men. And then, we're going to sit at the top, and we're going to eat some turkey."

Thanksgiving. He'd forgotten that it was Thanksgiving. Forgotten that everyone back in the World was sitting around, overeating, complimenting aunts on their marshmallow-yam casseroles, and then, lounging around in front of the television, or going on over to the high school to watch the Homecoming game. He'd forgotten all about that.

The artillery prep had already begun — rounds coming from every firebase within miles, and slamming into the hill, fifty or sixty at a time. For an hour.

By 0700, the air strikes had begun, and they could actually see trees flying up in the air like toothpicks. It ended at 0813, by Michael's watch, and at precisely 0814, they moved out and up the trail.

Up the hill.

CHAPTER 15

IT WASN'T RAINING, so much as misting. Michael had gotten so he barely noticed anymore. The first bunker complex they hit was empty, and had obviously taken more than a few direct hits.

Good.

They moved slowly up the trail, in a long column, the jungle violently torn away in patches around them, bomb craters everywhere. It was quiet. Too quiet, really. The air was so thick with the smells of cordite and napalm that it was hard to breathe.

The going was steeper now — they were already further than they had gotten the day before — and when they came to a trench line, word passed back for everyone to hold in place. Like everyone else, Michael dropped down to one knee — his good knee — and waited. Nobody said a word. He had no idea what 2nd Platoon was seeing up there, but artillery was called in, and he figured they were softening up the area ahead — just in case. Maybe the contact Bravo Company had had the night before really *had* been the NVA leaving. Cutting their losses.

Didn't seem likely.

They were moving again, right behind the artillery attack — and somehow, when the NVA opened up on them from yet another bunker complex, Michael wasn't surprised. He was scared, and lying flat on the ground like everyone else — but, he wasn't surprised.

The officers were yelling for them to spread out, to advance on line, and they were all returning fire, crawling up the hill a foot at a time. And falling back, two feet at a time.

"Grazing fire!" Sergeant Hanson was yelling. "Skip it into the bunkers!"

Michael concentrated on firing lower — it was easy to fire too high, especially on hills — and low fire, even if it just ricocheted off the ground, had a much better chance of connecting with something. Some*one*.

People. He was trying to kill *people,* actual living — *don't* think about it. Think of them as — robots. That's how they fought, anyway. And — they were the enemy. And — Communism was bad.

He laughed weakly, keeping his head down

behind a splintered log. That's why he was here. When he should be home, eating turkey, and fighting with Dennis and Carrie about who was going to do the dishes. Because some big shots somewhere thought that Communism — a concept he would probably have trouble defining on a social studies test — was bad. He, personally, didn't care if they were godless Communists — as long as they left *him* alone.

"Concentrate your fire!" someone — Lieutenant Brady? — was yelling. "Let the .90s work!"

Only — nothing seemed to be working on the bunkers — not grenades, or LAWs, or even the recoilless rifles — and despite the shrapnel and bullets flying everywhere, knocking wood and rocks all over him, Michael felt a flash of admiration for whoever had built the damned things. Hours of artillery and air strikes, and they were still standing. And there were men still *in* there, fighting. Jesus Christ, maybe they *weren't* human.

Something clanged — hard — off the top of his helmet, and he was stunned when he realized that it was a stick-handled grenade, which kept bouncing down the hill behind him. He covered his head defensively — *way* after the fact — and the grenade went off, maybe twenty meters down, and a second later, he heard a scream.

Oh, God. It was meant for him, and it got someone else. He was going to go back to help, but someone pushed him forward.

"Keep moving!" the guy yelled. "Don't stop!"

Michael had no idea who he was, or if he knew what he was talking about, but he kept moving. Crawling. The NVA soldiers were rolling more grenades down the hill, and they bounced crazily, off people, and *on* people, and exploding seemingly at random.

He used both hands, trying to dig a hole, to try and get out of the way, but everyone was still pushing forward — so, he had to, too.

"Backblast!" the recoilless rifle guys kept yelling, and then, they would fire again. Anyone who got caught behind one of the rifles when they fired didn't have a whole lot of chance of surviving. The concussion alone had killing force. Despite all that power, it looked like most of the rounds were impacting harmlessly on top of the dirt-covered bunkers. Seemed like they were covered with about ten *feet* of dirt. Those damned NVA were taking this war *seriously*.

Michael fired off short bursts, keeping his rifle on semiautomatic, trying to conserve his ammunition, and crawling up the hill. He wanted to throw grenades — but, he didn't want to waste them, either.

Someone was shouting for them to lay down covering fire, and he saw someone else scrambling up the hill, running to throw grenades into the side of the nearest A-frame bunker. Looked a hell of a lot like Finnegan — and it seemed like an incredibly brave and stupid thing to do. He fragged the hell out of the bunker, diving down to escape the force of the blast, then flipped a couple more grenades into the next closest bunker. It exploded, with an almost immediate secondary explosion. Ammo. The NVA must have had a hell of a lot of ammo stored in there. Not anymore.

Everyone was charging forward now, pouring fire into the bunker line, and he could see people doing crazy-heroic things like a guy standing right in front of a bunker, spraying it with his M-60, then leaping inside to go after whoever might have survived.

Guys around him were falling, and he wasn't sure if it was because they were hurt, or because they had just plain tripped. There was so much torn-up *stuff* all over the ground, and his knee hurt so much, that he was falling practically every other step. But, he would pick himself up, and keep charging, snapping magazines in and out of his gun as fast as he could. Only — it jammed. He was firing like crazy one second, and the next second — it wouldn't fire at all.

Fuck! Oh, *fuck*. He threw himself down behind what was left of a tree, and hit the gun as hard as he could, trying to knock the magazine out. It was stuck. The whole *thing* was stuck. Useless.

Fuck! Now what? He rolled onto his back behind the tree, not sure what to do. It was raining. It was raining harder than it had been before. Guys were charging up the hill, yelling at the tops of their lungs, some of them falling, and other guys climbing right up over them.

Jesus Christ. This was out of control. He had to do something. What was he going to do? A big clot of debris came flying into his lap — okay, right into his *crotch* — and he screamed, trying to brush it off, thinking it was shrapnel. Rocks. It was only rocks and dirt. But he wasn't going to stay around here and wait for them to get lucky.

He rolled onto his stomach, looking around. There was a collapsed bunker off to his left, and he grabbed a frag from his web gear, heading for it. He threw it in, flung himself down to wait for the explosion, then climbed inside, looking for a weapon. There were bodies, and pieces of bodies, all piled on top of one another, and he ripped an AK-47 out of one of the dead soldiers' hands, grabbed what had to be an ammo pouch, and rolled up out of the bunker just in time to see some guy charging towards him, brandishing his rifle. It happened too fast for Michael to yell out a warning, but the guy stopped just in time, firing the burst of M-16 fire straight up into the air instead.

"Asshole! I almost wasted you!" the guy yelled, and didn't wait for an answer, scrambling up and over the bunker.

Jesus. Hadn't even had time for his life to flash before his eyes. Probably didn't happen, anyway. And — he didn't particularly want to find out for sure. He shook his head, hard, to recover himself, then checked the bolt action of the AK-47. Seemed like it worked all right. So he got up, and climbed over the bunker himself, and saw the guy who had almost killed him lying a few feet up the hill, bleeding. A grenade, looked like. He hadn't even made it ten more feet.

Was he alive? Michael couldn't tell if he was alive, but he pulled the pressure bandage from his helmet band, pressing it on his chest, where the most blood was, trying to stop the flow.

"Doc!" He yelled. Could anyone hear him? He took a deep breath and yelled louder. "*Doc!*"

A medic he didn't know came running up, dropping down next to him in the mud.

"I got it," he panted. "Keep going!"

Right. Michael nodded, hesitated, then slung the AK-47 over his shoulder and took the guy's M-16. It might be self-preservation, but he felt like an animal. A monster. Only the poor guy sure as hell wasn't going to be using it anymore. The magazine was empty, and he reloaded, then climbed a few feet higher, shooting wherever it seemed like he was supposed to be shooting.

The hill was getting muddy. Hard to climb. And his left leg wasn't much help at all.

"Ammo up!" a voice was shouting. A familiar voice. Viper.

Michael looked around, then located him behind some rocks, sending out a stream of fire and tracer rounds from his .60, on a bunker up ahead. Michael crawled over, pulling off the two belts of ammo he'd been carrying around his chest.

"Link 'em up!" Viper yelled. "Then, feed me!"

Michael did it, working as fast as he could, turning to yell "Ammo up! We need ammo for the pig!" down the hill. These two fresh belts weren't exactly going to last long.

"Where's Snoopy?" he yelled. "Is Snoopy okay?"

"Haven't seen him!" Viper yelled, firing nonstop.

Someone higher up the hill — Hanson? maybe — yelled "Guns up!", and Viper grabbed the barrel of the .60 with his already bandaged hand and went tearing up the hill towards the voice.

Michael didn't know what else to do, so he followed him up into a trench.

"Here they come!" someone yelled.

"They're flankin' us, man!" someone else yelled. "Hit the flank!"

A wave of NVA was storming down the hill towards them, and for a second, Michael was too scared to do more than stare. Everyone who was in the trench was returning fire, and a lot of the NVA soldiers were dropping, but the guys who weren't in the trench and were out in the open were falling almost as fast.

It was sheer point-blank fire for — Michael didn't know how long — long enough for his new M-16 to heat up and then jam, and for him to have to switch to the AK-47 — and the wounded guys who could, dragged themselves to the trench, tumbling inside, dragging most of the others, who couldn't, with them.

"Pull back!" someone who sounded like Lieutenant Brady ordered. "Pull back *now*!"

"We got 'em, man!" someone else yelled. "We're almost there!"

"I said, pull back!" Lieutenant Brady yelled. "They'll cut us apart!"

It was more of a melee than a retreat as they pulled back behind the bunkers they had already taken, to regroup. A lot of guys were hurt, screaming for medics, or their mothers, or just plain screaming, and corpsmen scurried around, trying to take care of them. An air strike came in, destroying what was left of the top of the hill, Michael pushing as deep into the mud as he could, trying to get away from the explosions or, at least, the noise. The ground shook so much that it felt like the whole damned hill was just going to break to pieces. And his eardrums were going with it.

He was beyond scared. Beyond terror, beyond being paralyzed. All he wanted to do was run screaming down the hill and — he couldn't take it, he was going to completely, fucking lose his — he didn't want to die. He *really* didn't want to die.

"Let's go!" Sergeant Hanson yelled. "Move out!"

Michael took a deep breath, closed his eyes tightly, and started crawling up the hill.

Again.

CHAPTER 16

ADVANCE, RETREAT; advance, retreat. Mud and rain, and guys screaming and falling and dying all over the place. Shooting, and explosions, and noise, and more noise.

It was past 0330, and they were pinned down again in some muddy, body-crowded trench. Some of the bodies were alive, and some of them weren't. Some of the ones that weren't were American, and some of them were Vietnamese.

"*No* gunships!" a lieutenant he'd never seen before was yelling into his radio. "We've got a whole platoon still up there! Over!"

There were helicopters cruising around in the sky — some were Cobra assault choppers and the like, but others were LOHs — light observational helicopters — and C & Cs, which were Command and Control. In other words, where generals and other Army brass sat to enjoy the

208

show, and pretend that the blood and death was just one big chess game.

The platoon — what was left of them — was maybe one hundred meters up, near the top of the hill, pinned down in place. The NVA above them seemed to be taking their time, picking them off one by one, and it was so sadistic that it made Michael sick to watch. They had to either go up and get them, or go up and *join* them.

He looked around, to both sides, but didn't see anyone he knew. Didn't even see anyone who looked *familiar*. Oh, God — what if that was *his* platoon up there? Everyone was so separated and confused by now that he had no idea where any of them were.

But he sure as hell couldn't stand crouching down here and watching.

"Fuck this, man," he said to the filthy, dazed-looking guy next to him, and burst up out of the trench, running up the hill, dropping and shooting as he went, taking cover any damn place he could find it. *Making* his knee respond.

"Lay down some fire for that idiot!" he heard someone screaming.

He kept running and diving, with no idea whether anyone was following him, looking for an antenna. That would mean an RTO, and where there was an RTO, you could generally find a lieutenant. Or *someone* in authority.

He threw himself down into the middle of the group of guys. Completely unfamiliar guys. Maybe Delta Company, maybe the 3/21. Maybe even Alpha. Did it matter?

"Move up!" he yelled. "Up here!" He ran again, firing all the way, and most of them followed. To his amazement. They were all slightly less exposed now, behind a mound of mud, and he crawled over to a trembling RTO who had a lot of acne.

"Where's your L-T?" he demanded.

The kid pointed towards a body back down the hill.

Oh, great.

A voice crackled over the radio. "Charlie Two-Six, this is Sky-Six, please respond. I need a sit-rep. Over."

Sky-Six. Some damned general up above them. Michael grabbed the phone. "Sky-Six, we got a little problem here," he said. "Uh — Over."

"I don't want to hear it!" the voice came crackling back. "You take your men, Two-Six, and you take this hill! Over."

Jerk. "Yeah, well, why don't you come down *here,* and tell me that," Michael said.

"Who is this?" the voice crackled. "Identify yourself, soldier!"

At the moment, he was probably the Voice of Reason. "Who's *this*?" he asked.

Someone grabbed the radio-telephone out of his hand. "Sky-Six, this is Echo Three-Six," he said. "Wait one for sit-rep. Over."

Lieutenant Kendrick. His favorite officer in the world.

A very bad day had just gotten worse.

"Get on line with the others, private, I'll — " Kendrick stopped, recognizing him. "Oh, shit."

His sentiments, exactly. "Yeah, I'm happy to see you, too," Michael said. Thrilled.

Not that this was a great time for the two of them to have it out again.

Lieutenant Kendrick must have agreed, because he turned to the others. "All right, men," he said. "We can't stay here, so on my signal, we're going to assault."

That was stupid. Michael looked around. Was he the only one who thought that was stupid? They would be lucky if they made it twenty feet.

"*You*," Lieutenant Kendrick said. "Get on line."

Not a chance. Michael didn't move, except to duck a shower of mud. The NVA soldiers were

starting to figure out where they were, and the
RPGs and grenades were coming again, most of
them landing just on the other side of the mound
they were behind. Very close for comfort.

"*Now,*" Lieutenant Kendrick said.

His head hurt. His *knee* hurt. They were going
to run up there, and they were going to get blown
away. Michael rubbed his hand across his face.
He was so tired. And he was about to die on a
stupid muddy hill with a number for a name.

The radio crackled. "Echo Three-Six, what is
your sit-rep. Over."

Lieutenant Kendrick picked up the radio handset. "I just *got* here — I'm trying to find out the
sit-rep. Hold on. Over." He glared at Michael.
"Get on line. I'm not going to tell you again."

Get on line, and die. Happy Thanksgiving. Michael rubbed his eyes, only managing to get more
dirt in them, trying to think. He *really* didn't
want to die.

"Rifles up!" Lieutenant Kendrick ordered.
"On three, we — "

"Fake pass," Michael said, suddenly.

Lieutenant Kendrick looked over. His eyes
were bloodshot and surrounded by mud, too.
"What?"

Dumb jock. The thing to do, was talk at his

level. "Flea-flicker," Michael said. "Statue of Liberty. Ring any bells, college boy?"

Lieutenant Kendrick moved his jaw, then looked at the others. "Grenades," he said. "Don't just *sit* here!"

Everyone else started throwing grenades, over the mound, in case the NVA soldiers were advancing. No one was about to stand up and *look*.

"Call an air strike," Michael said. "Two pairs, two passes. Only — don't have them drop anything. While those sons-of-bitches have their heads down, we'll move in."

"What are you, a fucking tactician?" Lieutenant Kendrick asked, his jaw still jutting. Big, square, red-faced jaw.

"Got a better idea, college boy?" Michael asked.

Lieutenant Kendrick thought about that for a bare second, then got on the radio.

The plan, it developed, was for them to attack right after the first pair headed in, and everyone down the hill would be assaulting right behind them. Sky-Six seemed enthusiastic, exhorting them to *take* the damn hill.

He was scared. It was hard to breathe. He checked his rifle — his fifth? sixth? — of the day. If he got lucky, maybe it would work. If not, he still had some grenades, a .9mm automatic pistol he'd gotten off an NVA body, and his knife. If it came down to it, he would start throwing rocks. Do his best to bean them off the head. He had a good arm; he'd played center field. No problem.

The jets were coming. He could hear them coming. Help.

"Now!" Lieutenant Kendrick yelled.

They stormed over the mound, fragging, and shooting, and fragging some more. It was fast, and furious, and Michael was screaming obscenities he didn't even know he *knew*. And he knew plenty.

Everyone else was going just as wild as he was, and he went up and up the hill, fragging bunkers and shooting all the way, until there didn't seem to be any place else to go. He was out of magazines, so he yanked the pistol out of his web gear and whirled around, holding a grenade in the other hand. He whirled around — and around — looking for something else to shoot. Something else to frag. Something to *do*.

Except — he was on the top of the hill. The whole platoon — what there was of it — was at the top of the hill, and there didn't seem to be any NVA left. Didn't seem to be *anything* left.

He whirled around, and around, still pumped up, checking everything that moved. Americans. All he could see was Americans. Filthy, dirty, exhausted, beautiful Americans.

"Perimeter!" Lieutenant Kendrick yelled. "Secure it!"

Some people responded; some people didn't, but it didn't really seem to matter. It was over. Unbelievable as it seemed, it was over. Guys still coming up the hill were blowing and sealing bunkers, checking to make sure that there weren't any enemy soldiers left, but — it really was over.

Over.

Some guys were shouting things to each other and hugging and celebrating; some guys were wandering around in a daze; some guys just collapsed right where they were, in complete exhaustion.

Michael just stood there, not sure what to do. What to think. How to feel. Slowly, he bent the pin on his frag, and put it back on his web gear. Then, he looked around, decided it was safe, and stuck the pistol in the waistband of his very muddy and torn pants. And stood there.

Lieutenant Kendrick was standing nearby, and they looked at each other. Kendrick was muddy and torn-up, too.

"I still don't think I like you," Kendrick said, finally.

Michael nodded. "I don't like you, either."

Kendrick nodded too, and came over to stand next to him. If they were friends, they would have leaned on each other. They didn't.

"You're a little prick," Kendrick said, "but if I liked you better, I think I'd write you up for a medal."

A medal. Michael looked around at the devastation around him, bleeding guys being helped down the hill, others still lying where they'd fallen. Guys who weren't going to be getting up again. "Think I'd just as soon you didn't like me," he said.

Kendrick nodded.

They stood there, watching, too tired to move.

"You can be my RTO anytime, kid," Lieutenant Kendrick said, then went down to supervise some guys who were trying to collapse one last stubborn bunker.

Kid. Michael looked around. Bloody bandages, discarded weapons, dud rounds, empty ammo cans, what was left of the trees, mud. Lots of mud.

His squad. He had to find his squad. Had to find his friends. Had to find Snoopy.

He limped around the top of the hill, his legs

so weak and shaky they didn't want to support him, passing group after group of guys sitting down, staring at nothing. Guys he didn't know.

He was starting to panic, when he saw Viper, leaning up against part of a tree, smoking. Then — he saw all of them, on the ground near the tree. Viper, Sergeant Hanson, Jankowski, Finnegan — and Snoopy must be — Snoopy wasn't there.

He stood very still, his heart seeming to stop inside of his chest. Christ, no. Not *Snoopy*. Oh, God.

Jankowski saw him first, then they all looked up, dully, obviously too tired and drained to move. Michael couldn't move, either, feeling a blast of such grief that he couldn't do anything but stand where he was, and stare back at them.

Sergeant Hanson moved first, much slower than usual, turning to look over his shoulder. "Hey," he called, his voice raspy and barely recognizable. "He's over here."

Michael saw the tilted helmet first, coming around the side of a tree, and then — Snoopy. Covered with mud, a big grin on his face.

"Hey, there, Georgy Girl," he said cheerfully. " 'Bout *time* you showed up."

Michael came so close to bursting into tears

that he had to sit down. Immediately; his legs almost giving out beneath him.

"No, man, over here." Snoopy came over and gave him a hand up, Michael still so close to crying that he felt like slugging him. "Come on." Snoopy led him over to a log near the others. "Here you go, you just sit yourself down right here."

Michael sat down. He looked around, feeling dizzy, seeing that all of them were pretty filthy and banged up, but definitely only walking wounded. Finnegan looked the worst, a bloody bandage wrapped around his right shoulder and upper chest. Michael looked at him, worried.

Finnegan shrugged, then winced. "Ti-ti shrapnel. It's a skate."

Right. Sure. But — nobody was running screaming for a medic, so it must not be *too* serious.

He was too tired to speak, or move, but he looked around a little, for people he knew. He saw Lieutenant Brady and the Company CO standing together, conferring — so, that was good. Other than that, everyone looked too muddy and slumped over to be familiar — and he was too tired to deal with it, anyway.

Viper handed him a cigarette, and he nodded, having to think to remember how to smoke it.

Think hard. Snoopy was still kind of bouncing around, but the rest of them just stayed where they were, resting. Recovering.

Then, Doc came hustling over, half of his uniform torn off, as though he had been using it for bandages at some point. He looked at all of them rapidly.

"You okay? Everyone okay?" he asked.

They all nodded.

"Sit down, man," Snoopy said. "Take it easy."

Doc shook his head, his shoulders very hunched up and tense. Quivering a little. "I can't — I gotta check everyone, make sure everyone's okay. I got *ree*-sponsibilities, gotta take care of 'em." He pointed at Finnegan. "You get back down to the CP. *Soon*." Then, he hurried off.

It was quiet again. Michael, for one — even if he'd had the energy — could think of absolutely nothing to say.

"So," Snoopy said. "What *I* think, is that we need a snack. A little snack, and we'll all be jim-dandy again." He fumbled in one of the envelope pockets in his jungle utility pants, pulling out a C-rat can. With a bullet hole in it. "*Damn,*" he said. "They shot up my snack." He frowned for a second, then grinned, reaching into another pocket. "Luckily," he said, "I brought two." He grinned at all of them. "Turkey loaf? Anyone?"

Turkey loaf. What else? Michael laughed, weakly. He wasn't the only one.

"Sounds like a yes," Snoopy said, "from all of my little friends." He took the P-38 hanging from his dog tag chain, and started opening the can, promptly cutting his finger on the lid. "Ow. *Damn*," he said, then held his finger up. "Sarge? Purple Heart?"

Sergeant Hanson shook his head, but he was starting to smile. They all were.

"So, come on." Snoopy dug a very filthy, broken plastic spoon out of his pocket. "Let's have some turkey loaf."

Cold wet muddy turkey loaf. It was, after all, a holiday.

"Sounds good," Sergeant Hanson said, and Viper nodded, coming to sit down with the rest of them.

"Sounds *real* good," Finnegan said.

Jankowski moved over on his log to make room for Viper. "Sounds great."

Michael nodded, and reached out for the spoon. "Me, first," he said.

GLOSSARY

AIT: Advanced Infantry (or Individual) Training

AK-47: Soviet-made automatic assault rifle, used by NVA and VC troops

AO: Area of Operations

Article 15: disciplinary action taken against a soldier, usually because of insubordination; much less serious than a court martial

ARVN: Army of the Republic of Vietnam (South Vietnam)

B-rations: reconstituted food rations

Boonie hat: soft-brimmed hat

Boonierat: slang for infantry soldier

Boonies: slang for being out in the field

The bush: slang for being out in the field

C-4: plastic explosive

C & Cs: Command and Control; the helicopters in which unit commanders fly, in order to observe battles from above

Charlie: slang for Viet Cong

Cherry: slang for new, inexperienced soldier

Chi-Com: abbreviation for Chinese Communist; also, slang for wooden-handled — often highly unreliable — grenades, used by the VC and NVA, manufactured in China

Chinooks: large cargo helicopters; also known as CH-47s

Chop-chop: slang for food

Claymore mine: antipersonnel mine (US-made; hundreds of tiny steel balls propelled forward by a charge of plastic explosive upon detonation)

Cobra (also called *snake*): an assault helicopter, with heavy armament; officially known as the AH-1G

Commo shack: slang for communications bunker; where highly sophisticated radio and other vital communications equipment is situated, always under heavy protection

CP: Command Post

C-rations: canned combat rations, eaten in the field

CS: tear gas, usually referring to a tear gas grenade

DEROS: Date of Estimated Return from Overseas

Deuce-and-a-half: two-and-a-half-ton truck; used for transport

Didi: Vietnamese for "go quickly" or run

Dink: derogatory slang referring to Viet Cong; often referred to *any* Vietnamese person

Dinky-dau: Americanized version of Vietnamese expression for "crazy"

DMZ: Demilitarized Zone; a narrow strip of land dividing North Vietnam from South Vietnam

Door-gunner: soldier who sits in the bay of a helicopter, firing his gun in an attempt to protect the helicopter and crew

Dust-off: emergency medical evacuation by helicopter; also, the helicopter itself

Eleven-Bravo: MOS for an infantryman

EM Club: Enlisted Men's Club

Entrenching tool: small, collapsible shovel

EOD: Explosive Ordnance Disposal

FDC: Fire Direction Control; the center from which artillery missions are controlled; sometimes referred to as Fire Directional Control, or Fire Direction Center

Firebase (also, *FSB, Fire Support Base*): an artillery battery set up to provide fire support to units out in the field; sometimes, firebases are permanent, and other times, they exist only temporarily, before being torn down and relocated

Flechette: an artillery round (also used in recoilless rifles) with extreme destructive power; filled with shrapnel or sharp metal darts that spread out in a devastating spray upon detonation

Frag grenade: fragmentation hand grenade, carried by soldiers

Freedom bird: slang for plane returning soldiers to the United States at the end of their tours

GI: slang for soldier; officially — government issue

Gook: derogatory slang for the Viet Cong and NVA; often, used for all Vietnamese

Grunt: slang for infantryman, or boonierat

Gunship: combat attack helicopter; will assault suspected or confirmed enemy positions to assist soldiers in the field

HE: High Explosive (referring, generally, to an artillery round; sometimes, an M-79 grenade)

Heat tabs: inflammable tablets, provided to heat C-rations in the field; not always effective

H & I: Harassment and Interdiction fire; harassing barrage of artillery fire sent in direction of suspected enemy locations

Hootch: bunker or tent, used as shelter for military personnel; also, used to describe dwelling where villagers live

Howitzer (105mm): standard artillery piece (gun); its fire missions are used to support troops in the field

HQ: headquarters

Huey (also called *slick*): a UH-1 helicopter, used most commonly for troop transport

Hump: carrying a heavy load while marching on patrol

I Corps: the northernmost military region of South Vietnam

K-bar: military knife

KIA: Killed in Action; sometimes, stated by military code — Kilo-India-Alpha

Klick: kilometer

KP: Kitchen Police; a work detail in the kitchen; generally given as punishment for minor infractions

LAW: Light Antitank Weapon; also known as M-72

LBJ: Long Binh Jail (the stockade for military personnel in Vietnam)

Lifer: derogatory reference to career soldiers

LOHs: Light Observation Helicopter; flies above the battlefield; pronounced "Loach"

LP: Listening Post

LRRP: Long Range Reconnaissance Patrol; also, refers to the members of said patrol; pronounced "Lurp"

LSA: Lubricant, Small Arms

LZ: Landing Zone (for helicopters)

M-16: lightweight automatic/semiautomatic machine gun, weighing 7.6 pounds when loaded; rifle used by American infantrymen

M-60: American machine gun, fed by belt of

ammunition; the gun weighs twenty-three pounds, unloaded

M-79: grenade launcher; called "thumper" or "bloop gun," due to the sound it makes when firing

MACV: Military Assistance Command Vietnam

Mad minute: a free-fire practice and test session for weapons

Magazine: holds twenty rounds (bullets) and is inserted into the M-16

Medevac: medical evacuation by helicopter; dust-off

Mermite: heavily insulated containers used to transport hot food to soldiers in the field

Mike: slang for minute; also, the military phonetic abbreviation for the letter M

Mike-mike: slang for millimeter

MOS: Military Occupational Specialty

MPC: Military Payment Certificate; currency used by American forces in Vietnam

NCO: Noncommissioned Officer

NDP: Night Defensive Position

Number one: slang for "the best"

Number ten: slang for "the worst"

NVA: North Vietnamese Army (the enemy)

OCS: Officer Candidate School

OD: olive drab

OP: Observation Post

P-38: small metal can opener used to open C-rations

PFC: Private First Class

Point: the lead man in a patrol

Post Exchange (also, *PX*): store located on military bases where soldiers can purchase a wide variety of items; often, prices are much lower than they are in nonmilitary stores

Pot (also, *steel pot*): slang for helmet

PRC-25: infantry radio carried by RTOs in the bush to maintain communication with the rear

Probe: used to describe the way the enemy can mount an attack, generally at night; brief and tentative, as opposed to a full frontal assault

PZ: Pick-up Zone (troop and/or medevac extraction)

Quonset hut: military structure for office and other facilities on a military base; easy to assemble and take apart; made of curved, corrugated metal

R & R: Rest and Relaxation

The rear: anyplace where noncombat support troops are located

Rock and roll: firing a weapon on full automatic

RPG (also *B-40*): rocket-propelled grenades, used by enemy forces, fired from the shoulder

RTO: Radio-Telephone Operator

Saddle up!: order commonly given to troops at

rest, indicating for them to resume marching

S & D: Search and Destroy; a mission during which troops locate, and destroy, anything the enemy might be able to use — food, weapons, shelter

Sapper: an enemy soldier who would try to infiltrate the perimeter, heavily armed with explosives

Satchel charge: bags of explosives carried by sappers, used for large-scale demolition during a surprise attack; a bag would, for example, be tossed into a bunker, destroying it upon detonation

Sit-rep: situation report

A skate: an easy day, mission, or task, as in "It's a skate."

Slack: the person who walks behind the point man on patrol

Smoke grenade: grenades carried by soldiers, which emit smoke in various colors; used for signaling

Snake and Nape: slang for heavy air support, involving the use of both napalm and gunships

SOP: Standard Operating Procedure

Stand-to: phrase used to describe the tight, defensive perimeter formed by a unit, all personnel in a circle, facing out, while they receive instructions from the officer in charge

Ti-ti: slang for "small"

TOC: Tactical Operations Center

Tracer: bullet, or round, with phosphorus on it; as the bullet is fired, the phosphorus burns, creating a visual track of the bullet's flight; generally, every fifth round is a tracer; particularly useful for night fighting

Viet Cong (also *VC, Victor Charlie*): Vietnamese Communist; it refers to the National Liberation Front, which is the organization of South Vietnamese Communists who were fighting against the American troops and the ARVN; the Viet Cong were under either direct, or unofficial, control of the North Vietnamese Army

Ville: slang for village

Wake-up: last day of a soldier's tour before being sent home, as in "ten days and a wake-up"

Web gear: suspenders and belt a soldier wears to which necessary equipment can be attached, and reached more easily in an emergency (web gear, as opposed to less essential gear, which would be stored in a soldier's rucksack)

White phosphorus (also *WP, Willy Pete, Willie Peter*): refers to an incendiary artillery round, generally used for marking a target, but also very destructive; can also be used in grenades

WIA (also, *Whiskey-India-Alpha*): Wounded in Action

The World: any place *other* than Vietnam; more
    specifically, the United States
XO: Executive Officer

Look for ECHO COMPANY #3:
'Tis the Season, coming soon . . .

It was beginning to look a lot like Christmas. That is, if Christmas could be rainy, and hot, and full of blood, and pain, and death — and in Vietnam. There was something too depressing about carols, under the circumstances, so Rebecca walked around the ward singing, "Ten Cents a Dance," instead. Made TPRs seem so much more cheery.

Besides — it was one of the songs she did best.